Copyright © 2(

Matt Shaw Publications

The moral right of Matt Shaw to be identified as the author of this work has been asserted in accordance with the Copyright, Designs and Patents Act, 1988. All Rights reserved. No part of this publication may be reproduced or transmitted in any form or by any means, electronic or mechanical, including photocopy, recording or any information storage and retrieval system, without permission in writing from the publisher.

A CIP catalogue record for this book is available from the British Library.

ISBN-13: 978-1500682606

ISBN-10: 1500682608

This book is a work of fiction. Names, characters, businesses, organisations, places and events are either the product of the author's imagination or are used fictitiously. Any resemblance to actual persons, living or dead, events or locales is entirely coincidental.

PORN

MATT SHAW

OUR LAST SHOOT

I slipped the tight latex hood over my head and secured the ball-gag in place; ball in mouth - held there by leather strap round the head - and fastened at the back. I checked my reflection out in the broken mirror hanging on the wall. I felt sick. Memories came flooding back to me. Memories which I'd sooner forget. I walked from the back room where I'd gotten changed into my latex catsuit. It felt weird putting it on. I hadn't worn it since that shoot. Lucky I still had it. Part of me had wanted to burn it after that night, and I nearly did, but I'm glad I hadn't. Had I done so - I wouldn't have been able to wear it now. I wouldn't have been able to see the look on his face when he finally sees me dressed up. I wonder if he'll remember the relevance of the outfit. I do hope so. I don't want to have to explain it.

The sound of my high-heeled thigh high's hitting the cold concrete of the warehouse floor alerted him to my presence as I approached him from behind. He was bound, naked, to one of the large concrete supports holding the high roof up and couldn't see me from this angle.

"Who's there?" he asked. Do I detect a quiver in his tone? I do hope so. I want him to feel everything I had felt and - of all the emotions I experienced that night - fear was definitely up there. Second only to pain. "Hello?" he called out. "Who's there?" I didn't reply. I just walked up until I was close behind him. "Come on, enough is enough. Very funny. You got me. Come on, who is it?" He tried to change his tact; tried pretending he wasn't afraid and that he knew this was nothing but a prank. I have news for him: This isn't a prank. His name is Harry. If you ask anyone in the industry who Harry is today, they'd tell you he is an adult film director. If you ask anyone tomorrow they'll tell you he was a film director.

Still out of his line of sight, I walked across the warehouse to where I'd dropped my bag of play-things. I grabbed it by the leather handles and walked back across the room - back towards him. I walked round the pillar and revealed myself. He looked at me. I could see him, straining to try and see who I was. I can see that, deep down, he knows exactly who I am. He just doesn't want to admit it.

"Do I know you?" he asked. "Come on, take the hood off. Let me see your face..."

I took the gag off and moved closer to him. I held the ball up to his mouth and pushed it in, despite his best efforts to spit it back out. A quick knee to his testicles ensured he behaved himself and - more importantly - opened his mouth wide enough for the ball to fit in easier. I secured it in place with the buckle. He tried to say something but his words were mumbled. I don't mind. I don't want to hear what he says. I don't want to hear him try and talk his way out of this. I don't want to hear anything but his screams. And his screams I want to hear all night long. I took a few steps away from him and unzipped my hood, at the back. I hesitated for a moment before I pulled it off and dropped it to the floor. His eyes went wide more or less immediately. Whether he knew who I was before I revealed my face or not - he definitely knows me now and that's despite my gaunt appearance. And - within the next ten minutes or so - he'll regret meeting me and he'll regret employing me.

"I see from your face you remember me," I said. "How have you been doing? Made any more films recently?" He shook his head. "I don't believe you. People like you, you don't stop. You just keep on going, keep pushing - anything to make money. And it doesn't matter who you hurt." He tried to say something but couldn't get his mouth around the gag. I wasn't disappointed. I don't want to hear what he has to say. I don't want him trying to get in my head. I don't want him trying to put me off from what I want to do. "Well I have to be honest - I haven't acted for a while. In fact, your film was one of the last films I made. I won't lie, times are hard. Money is starting to dry up, you know?" He tried to say something again. Something else to ignore. "I was thinking about branching out, you know? I was thinking about doing what you do. I have a good eye." He went to say something but - again - couldn't get his words out. No loss, I'm sure. "I reckon I could make some good films. In fact...I have a camera with me now. Maybe - as we're old friends - you'd like to help me?" I reached down into the large bag and pulled out a small camcorder. "I know it's not as impressive as the ones your team use but I still think it will do the job." I switched it on and opened the small view-finder screen. "Cool thing is, it has loads of different recording functions. You know, things like Night Vision for if you want to make a naughty film with someone during the night...I don't know - maybe someone unsuspecting. You could just stash the camera out of sight, in the corner of the room and let it film away. Look!" I flipped the screen around with a quick twist and moved closer so he could take a look at what I was seeing. "Night vision. What do you think? Pretty cool, huh?" I flipped the screen back the other way around and stepped back again, aiming the camera at my future star.

He was straining against the restraints I had used to bind him to the pillar. He can strain all he wants but he's going nowhere. Thick, heavy-duty chains - all looped around his bare legs and naked chest - secured at the back with heavier duty padlocks.

"I think I like the fact it films in High Definition best of all, though. Picks up all the little details. Little beads of sweat and," I pointed the camera towards his flaccid cock. I couldn't help but laugh, "It's okay," I told him, "it's cold in here. I'm sure the viewers will understand when they see the tape. And I'm positive that - when we start - we'll both start feeling a little hot under the collar." I pressed the record button on the back of the camcorder and - keeping it aimed at his penis - I reached down with my other hand and gently fondled his balls." I heard him sigh. I aimed the camera up to his face as I continued to grope him. He closed his eyes as though he was getting into it. Mind you, I didn't need to see his face to know he was enjoying my (so far) gentle touch. Slowly his penis started to stiffen. I couldn't help but wonder whether he believed this was the reason I had brought him here; I wanted to get him all to myself so I could give him a hand-job? Silly man.

Keeping the camera aimed at his face - to capture his soon-to-be-changing expression - I squeezed his testicles hard and couldn't help but laugh when I noticed how wide his eyes went. For a split second, I thought they were going to pop right out of his head. I released the pressure and he breathed an audible sigh of relief. Little does he know - the relief he feels now - it's to be short-lived. The fun will really start when I utilise the special toys I've brought with me. But first - before I can do anything fun - I need to set up the shot.

I reached down into my bag and fished out a small tripod, being extra careful not to accidentally reveal anything else I have in the bag. I don't want him to see what's coming. I don't want him to see the toys. Not until I am ready to use them. I walked backwards a bit and put the tripod on the hard floor, ensuring the legs were splayed out properly to stop it from toppling over. Once it was secure, I extended the neck to its full height. I put the camera on the top and attached it to the plate, with the little screw provided. A quick look in the view-finder showed that he's perfectly framed. Not bad for a first attempt. Not bad at all.

I walked back to where he was bound and gently ran my hand against his testicles again, "I'm sorry, baby, did that hurt?" I whispered. He tried to say something - no doubt begging for his release. Wasted words. "Let me kiss it better," I purred. I dropped to my knees and moved my mouth close enough for him to be able to feel my breath against his manhood. I looked up at his face. He was looking down at me. A hopeful look on his face. Did he really think I'd kiss it? Was he really that fucking stupid? With no warning, I slapped his penis hard and laughed at his pained groan. "You're a maggot!" I shouted at him. I stood up tall again so we were more or less face to face. I looked him right in the eye, "Did you know? I never meant to end up in this industry. I wanted to be a real actress..."

A FRESH YOUNG FACE

The casting agent looked at my passport to ensure I was over the legal age for his film. I squirmed in the seat across from his desk - not because I had anything to hide but because the passport picture was less than flattering; it was taken when I was just sixteen years old. It was my nineteenth birthday yesterday and I think it's fair to say, I grew into my looks. The man looked over at the picture and made a funny snort through his nose when he spotted the photograph. How to make a girl feel pretty. Without saying anything he stood up and walked across the room to where a photocopier was sitting. He lifted the lid and placed my passport down on the glass before closing the lid again. A quick press of the 'copy' button with his finger and two copies of my passport printed out into the paper tray. He lifted the lid and returned to the table where he handed me the passport back.

"Everything seems to be in order," he said.

"Thank you," I took the passport from him and slid it back into my handbag.

"My only concern is your age."

"I'm old enough."

He smiled. "Let me rephrase that: My only concern is your experience."

I shifted nervously in my seat. I'd tried to be brave when I went into the office. Tried to work my nerves out of my system as I patiently sat in the waiting area next door. Thought I had managed it too but clearly I hadn't.

"Do you have any experience on film?" he asked.

"I starred in a commercial when I was just six years old."

"Probably not the experience we're talking about."

He was referring to my sexual experience. I'd had a couple of long term partners since I was seventeen but - to answer his question - I hadn't any experience on film to speak of.

"So what do you like to do?" he asked.

"I play netball..."

"That's great. What do you like to do sexually? What do you like to do when you're in bed?"

I felt my face redden. I had known they'd be asking pointed questions when I agreed to come to the interview - having phoned the office after spotting the advert in the back of a casting paper 'Adult Actresses Sought' - but that didn't make me any less nervous, or shy about it. He picked a pen up from his table and started scribbling something down on a notepad which rested next to a particularly grubby looking keyboard. I felt myself shift in the seat again.

"I like to give a man pleasure," I said.

"Specifics?"

"Blow jobs?"

"Was that a question?"

"I like to give blow-jobs," I said with an air of authority in my voice, having taken a deep breath. "I've been told I have a good technique."

"Who told you that?"

"My boyfriend."

The man made another note on the pad. I tried to see what he was writing, by craning my head towards the paper whilst he was looking down, but couldn't make it out. I sat upright again when he looked back up from what he was doing.

"Ever had a man cum in your mouth?" he asked.

"Yes."

"Like it?"

"Yes." I laughed. So much nervous energy.

"Spit or swallow?" he asked. I didn't know how to answer. I had swallowed but, truth be told, it wasn't really for me. If I was going to be honest, I wasn't actually a fan of having it in my mouth - the end product that is. Everything up to that point was fine but the salty taste turned my stomach. "We don't actually get a lot of call for girls swallowing to be fair. Most of the time the directors like to see it dribble down from the mouth and chin. Sometimes he'd rather the money shot was even aimed at the breasts. Still best to put as much information down as possible though."

"Either," I told him.

He made a note. "What's your favourite position?"

I had a feeling he wasn't looking for the answer 'missionary'. Again, I felt my face redden. I couldn't help but wonder whether he was picturing me doing all of what we spoke about as though I were some dirty tramp out for a good time. I realised he needed an answer, "I like them all." It seemed like the safest option.

"You must have a favourite?"

"Doggy." It was the only other one I knew the proper technical name for. I think you also had cowgirl and reverse cowgirl but I felt they weren't 'dirty' enough for what he was looking for. He nodded and made another note. "But," I continued, "I do like them all."

"Anal?" he asked, ignoring what I said. When I didn't answer him immediately he continued, "Not everyone is looking for that but we need to ensure we put as much down on your profile as possible. The moment you start getting fussy about what you do, and won't do, well that's the moment people turn away from your profile. The more boxes ticked, the more calls received."

"I've never tried it," I said.

"Would you be willing?" he asked.

"I guess."

"Then we'll tick it."

I guess, if it's ticked and they ask, they'll all be professional about it so they'd be able to start me off gentle.

"What's your sexual orientation?"

"Bi-sexual." I didn't hesitate. I was heterosexual but the thought of going with another woman didn't repulse me so - if required - I'd venture there. I believe they called it 'gay for pay'. The man nodded and made another note.

"And what about D.P?" he looked me in the eye. I felt my face redden again and just stared back at him blankly; no idea what it meant. "Double penetration?" he asked.

"I've never tried it," I told him, feeling foolish for not know what he meant in the first place.

"Which links us back to - would you be willing?" he asked.

I shrugged, "I guess."

"Finally - how do you feel about bareback?"

I looked at him blankly.

"Sex without a condom."

"I'd rather not."

"The pay can be better," he said. I felt as though he was pressurising me into saying 'yes' but this was one thing I was adamant on; I didn't want to have unprotected sex. I didn't do it in my private life and I wasn't about to do it in film. Not for any amount of money.

I shook my head once more.

He smiled. "Okay, I think that's that bit sorted..." he scribbled a final note.

"I also act," I butted in. Acting was the sole reason I had moved to the city. I foolishly believed I'd find the work I was seeking by moving to the centre of the city, close to where the majority of the auditions seemed to be. I'd had some luck, with small roles, but nothing which offered steady work and - sometimes - I found myself working just for the 'experience'. It wasn't long before my cards were maxed out and I was getting final demands for various utilities (gas, water etc) and - soon after that - I found myself answering the seedier of the adverts. Anything to pay the bills.

"Okay, I'll be sure to make a note of it." He set his pen to one side. "Right, we just need to take some photographs," he stood up and pointed me towards the back of the office. A white drape was hanging in front of the dirty looking wall. In front of that - a camera was set up on a tripod. "If you'd just like to go and stand in front of the drape we can get started."

"What? Now?" He nodded as I nervously stood up and made my way to the drape. I turned and faced the camera. Standard pose? One hand on my hip, slightly turned to the camera, smile on my face? I adopted the pose.

"Just stand face on, please. Hands by your side."

I changed my position as per his request, "Do I smile?"

He clicked the camera's button to take the shot after shaking his head. I felt exposed, standing here, without even a smile on my face. It didn't feel natural. I tried my best to hide it. If he saw I wasn't comfortable with this - he'd probably realise I'd be the same on set despite my best intentions not to be.

"Okay, that's good." He looked up at me, "If you could please remove your clothes, we'll do a couple of naked shots."

I hesitated. I hadn't expected this. Stupid really. Just shows how naive I am to this business - this world even. I waited a moment to see if he was going to leave the room. He was fiddling with the camera, whilst waiting for me. Clearly he was going nowhere. I undid the belt around my waist and unbuttoned my jeans. I lowered them to my ankles and kicked them off until I was standing in front of the man in nothing but my top and white lacy panties. I pulled my top off and threw it onto the jeans. Black silky bra and white lacy panties. Class act.

"Okay. Ready." I told him.

He looked up and pointed to the bra and knickers, "Need to come off too, please. They need to see your body. Scars and all."

He watched as I removed both bra and panties. I blushed again. Don't think I've ever blushed so much in all my life. I shifted my weight from one leg to the other.

"You need to relax. Your nerves will show up on camera. If you look nervous - you won't get the bookings. Directors will be looking for professionals they can work with. They don't want someone they'll have to babysit through the process."

I tried my best to relax. It probably would have helped had I been able to smile at least but - like the first picture - he wanted it completely neutral. My heart was racing as I heard the camera 'click'. Another picture taken.

"And turn to your side."

I did as instructed. Another 'click'.

"And turn your back to me."

Another 'click'.

I started to panic as I wondered how far this process was going to go. Was he going to want me to have sex with him on camera? Is that how these interviews work?

"Okay. Good."

I turned around and saw that he was unscrewing the camera from the tripod.

"Are we finished?" I asked him. "Can I put my clothes back on?"

"Just a couple more shots needed," he said. He pulled the camera free from the tripod as soon as he was able to and pointed me towards a leather settee at the side of the office. "I just want you to kneel on there - on all fours," he said as he ushered me towards the settee. I walked over and did as I was told. Another surge of nervous energy rushed through me as I heard a 'click' from behind as he took a picture. "You have a nice pussy," he said, "should get some attention."

I closed my eyes as I half expected to feel his touch (or worse) against my skin. Nothing. I quietly breathed a sigh of relief as I heard him walk to the other side of the room. I turned round to see what he was doing. He was putting the camera back on the tripod.

"You can get dressed," he told me, "we're just about done."

I climbed off the leather settee and made my way to my pile of clothes. "That's it?" I asked.

"Yeah. I'll load the pictures up, fill in your profile and then send it around to people this afternoon. They're always looking for new talent so, if we're lucky, we might start hearing back soon."

"And you really think I have a chance at this?" I asked him. Part of me wanted him to say 'no' but another part of me knew he had to say 'yes'. If I were to be able to stay here, in the city, and not go home to mum and dad - I needed him to say 'yes' and I needed the work to come in fast.

"You have an innocent look about you," he said, "would work nicely in role-play scenarios; like school girls, daddy and daughter - that kind of thing. Popular at the moment." He paused, "How'd you feel about that kind of thing?" he asked.

* * * * *

Harry tried to speak around the ball-gag. Once again his words were muffled. I undid the buckle on the back and pulled the ball from his mouth before dropping it to the floor. It bounced twice, despite the leather strap, and rested by his foot.

"What the fuck has this got to do with me?" he asked.

It had nothing to do with him. I was just reminiscing. I guess I was trying to figure out at which stage I had lost my innocence. Whether it was there or on the first shoot - I'm not sure. Probably when I initially signed up with the agency. I remember leaving the office wondering if I'd ever hear from them again. So many stories of these agencies who charge an administrator's fee and then - that's it - you never hear from them again.

"That was your choice!" Harry pointed out.

Yes. It had been my choice. I, more than anyone else, am aware that it was my choice. But that's not to say I chose what happened to me. That was completely out of my control and not asked for. And what happened - on that night - that was his fault. He was the director after all.

"What do you want?" he asked. He started to strain against his restraints. Pointless. He continued regardless, "This is nothing to do with me!"

It was true. This part of my life - the early days of my career - was nothing to do with him. But I wanted to show him where I'd come from, where I'd got and where he (they) took me. I wanted him to see it all. I wanted him to truly understand what he had done to me and - to do that - I had to start at the beginning.

"Do you remember the first thing you ever filmed?" I asked him.

"Just let me go."

"I remember my first scene."

MY FIRST SCENE

A few days went by without so much as a missed call from
the agency that I had signed with and I was starting to feel as
though I'd wasted what little money I had. No job offers from
'normal' acting roles I'd applied for and no interviews for
'real' jobs - one of which being a waitress job in a cafe close
to my flat. In fact the only phone call I had taken all week
was one from my concerned mother. I hadn't spoken to her
for a week and she had started to panic; the need for
constant communication to reassure her that I was safe and
well. She asked how things were going and, before I knew it, I
found myself lying.

"Things are going well," I had told her before going into
various roles I was currently working on (despite not actually
doing any of them for real).

When the phone did ring with a local number, my heart
skipped a beat before I'd even answered it. I knew who it
was. Don't ask me how, I just knew. I answered it with a
press of a button and held the phone - nervously - to my ear.
It was my agent; the man who had signed me up before
taking my photographs. He'd gone on to explain that a
producer had seen my photographs and was hoping to have
a chat with me. I asked him what that would entail and he
informed me that it would be an initial conversation before

filming a scene with one of the male actors. There was a promise of additional scenes if I got on okay with the first. Apparently the agent had informed the producer I was new to the industry and - although keen - I might not have what it took to do more than one scene. That was fine with me. I didn't want to find myself in a position where I'd be stuck with them for days if I didn't feel as though I was suited to the role. It was one thing in my imagination but to actually do it - for real - well that was something else entirely and only time would tell (and the cameras rolling) whether I was cut out for it.

"What do I have to do?" I had asked him.

He explained to me that that was what the initial conversation with the producer was for; a little chat about the film they were doing and the scenes they wanted to create. Apparently I'd be given a choice as to which scene I wanted to try out for. I just had to tell them what my limits were and they'd take it from there. Seemed fair enough. Especially when they informed me it would most likely be a couple of hours worth of work and I'd take home two hundred and fifty pounds in cash. I agreed to meet with the producer and was told a car would pick me up the following morning.

By the time morning had come round I hadn't slept a wink. All night I was plagued with thoughts as to whether I was doing the right thing. Questions popping into my head which - truthfully - should have come up sooner than the night before I was to be collected. Thoughts like - what if my mum and dad saw the films? What if their friends saw them and then told mum and dad about them. My parents (and their friends) didn't come across as the sort of people who'd venture out to watch an adult movie but - even so - it didn't stop the thought from being there in the forefront of my mind. I started to feel sick in the pit of my stomach as I tried to desperately put the thoughts from my mind. I'd be nervous enough, when I met the producer, and the last thing I need is the thought of mother and father bouncing around in my brain.

I think I had been gently dozing on the settee when there was a knock on the door, as the thumping noise - someone's fist against the wooden panels - startled me and made my heart race; a sensation which didn't stop when I realised what the noise was. If anything it raced harder. I jumped up from the settee and checked my reflection in the mirror hanging on the wall just above the electric fireplace. Thankfully I hadn't smudged my make-up whilst dozing and I still looked presentable for the upcoming meeting. I made my way through the small flat to the front door and opened it with the best possible smile I could muster up.

"Hi," I said - a bright smile beaming.

I wasn't sure whether the man standing in front of me was a driver or whether it was the actual producer. He was standing there, dressed in a black suit with a black tie and white shirt. I'd opted for a short skirt, a pair of heels and a crop top. I thought it made me look the part but looking at him - now I just felt like a dirty tramp; the kind of girl you'd usually see walking the walk of shame through the early hours of the morning, shoes in hand and cum leaking from her sordid encounter with yet another one night stand. It didn't help that I'd gone for typical 'porn-star' make-up too; heavy in order to hide every little blemish that the camera could have picked up on. If I was to go on film, I wanted to look my best.

The man smiled at me (I saw him clock what I was wearing) and said, "Victoria Sheldon?"

I nodded, "That's me." As if he didn't already know. How many other girls did he see dressed like this so early in the morning.

"I'm here to take you to meet Mr. Adams. If you'd like to follow me, the car is right this way."

He took a step back from the door, giving me the room to step from the safety of my flat. How I even managed to walk I don't know. My legs were like jelly.

* * * * *

"You've had your fun," Harry spat, "just let me go."

I hadn't even started 'my fun' yet.

"Do you know Richard Adams?" I asked him as he continued to tug against his restraints. Of course he knew him. It wasn't the name attached to the films he made - for that he had a stage name - but he had never made a secret about who he really was; a producer of one of the biggest adult film

23

companies in the UK. A true gentleman and a professional. Everything Harry wasn't.

"Of course I know him."

"He requested me, having seen my photos. Apparently he wanted to do a scene with me to see how I was on camera. The agency I signed with said - if I impressed him enough - I would get more scenes with him."

Harry was getting angrier by the minute, not that it mattered - he wasn't going anywhere, "Why are you telling me all of this?" he shouted.

I walked closer to him and whispered, "Because I want you to know what I had to do to get where I was when you found me," I purred. "Do you know what he made me do after an initial conversation?"

"Of course I don't fucking know!" Harry yelled.

"I had to take his man actor in my mouth and pleasure him until completion," I said. "I started by kissing him," I leaned forward and kissed Harry on the lips. I ran my hand across the bits of his chest not covered by chain. He wasn't shouting anymore. I kissed him softly again and even felt him pucker up for me. Another kiss for luck before I moved away (slightly), "I ran my hands over his body," I said as my hands continued to roam over Harry's body. My right hand tickled his inner thigh with my nails scratching across his skin gently. I caught his penis as I moved my hand and was pleased to see that - despite the situation he was in - it'd started to grow erect. "I remember how big he felt in my hand," I whispered as I took Harry in my own hand. "His sighs as I stroked him," I continued as my hand mirrored what I was describing by stroking Harry slowly. Up and down, up and down..." He sighed at the sensation of my delicate touch. I couldn't help but smile - not because of the pleasure I was giving him but more so because I knew it wasn't going to last. "When I felt he was hard enough..." I leaned in close to Harry's ear as I stroked him faster, "I got down on my knees and slid his cock between my wet lips.." Harry sighed - clearly aroused by the words and the touch. I kissed my way down his body until I was face to face with his pathetic cock. I closed my eyes - taking myself to a better place - and slid it into my mouth. Another sigh from Harry. Slowly, but firmly, I started to move my head backwards and forwards - listening closely to his reaction. After a couple of seconds I pulled away and let his cock slide from my mouth. "I was surprised at how easily I forgot anyone else was in the room. Just kept my eyes shut and got on with it - occasionally opening them to look up at his reaction to see if I was pleasing him. Of course, his eyes were closed - and his head tilted back against the settee we were on." I slid Harry's penis back in my mouth and started sucking. Harder and faster this time – let him have the false hope that I'd take him to the point of ejaculation. I looked towards the camera, still filming attached to the tripod at the side of us, and gave it a wink. A second later and I bit down. Not hard enough to do much damage - certainly not as hard I wanted to - but hard enough to cause him some pain. He screamed out loud as I pulled my mouth away. "You don't get to cum," I hissed, "I'm not finished with you."

* * * * *

The producer, Richard, had shouted 'cut' and the cameraman began packing the camera away. I was sitting on the edge of the settee in my underwear. My breasts lifted up over, and out of, my bra so my co-star had been able to get to my nipples - whether to tweak them or suck them; the choice was his.

My co-star - a pleasant (and good looking) man called Darren (not his working name) - was using a towel to clean my saliva and the remnants of his sperm from his penis. "You have a little bit on your chin," he smiled.

"What?" I raised my hand to my chin and - just as he'd informed me - felt a small amount of sperm hanging from there. I couldn't help but laugh as I wiped it off with the back of the same hand. "Thought I'd got it all," I laughed. "Can't believe how much there was!"

"Sorry about that," he laughed.

Richard was watching the file back on a laptop - having slotted the memory card into the card-reader. I looked, from where I was sitting, and saw he was at the end of the film - the money shot as they called it. "That was great," he said. He turned to Darren, "I take it you don't have any complaints?" he asked.

Darren shook his head, "Maybe we need to go for another take," he joked. "You know, just to be sure."

Richard turned his attention to me, "And how was it for you? Everything okay?"

I nodded, "I loved it." I actually did. I had worried all the previous night that I'd feel dirty after the shoot - used - but that wasn't the case. I didn't feel used and I didn't feel dirty. I felt great. I felt alive. More alive, in fact, than I'd felt for as long as I could remember. I knew - from a few moments into acting out the scene - that I'd made the right decision. This was the right call. This is what I wanted to do.

"Okay, well..." Richard paused a moment. You could tell from his face that he was still trying to make up his mind which direction to go in. I was waiting on tenterhooks for a decision. This is the man who could make or break me.

* * * * *

"Well you know how that day ended. Had it gone badly," I told Harry as he continued to whimper, "we would never have met." I laughed, "I bet you're wishing we'd never met now, aren't you?" I looked down at his softening cock; my teeth marks still visible. "He invited me back to film some more scenes."

"Why are you doing this to me?" He sounded pathetic. I could only hope the camera was close enough to hear his voice; hear how pathetic he was. So when it hit the web, when what I do to him goes viral - everyone will be able see how much of a pussy he was. "Just tell me. Why are you doing this to me?"

I sighed, "Because of what you did to me."

"I didn't do anything!"

"That's the problem. You didn't do anything. You didn't do anything yet you organised everything. What happened - you're to blame. It was your design. It was what you wanted. Just as this - and what happened to your colleagues - this is my design. This is what I want.

"I didn't know!" he insisted. Whether he knew about...him...That was by the by. The point was I was in that position because he forced me into it. Despite all my screams, my pleas for them to stop, he left the cameras rolling. He wanted them to capture it all. Just as I want this camera to catch all I'm about to do to him.

"Well soon you'll know everything. Which takes us to my name."

GETTING A NAME

"You don't want your real name in the credits," Richard told me as we sat down to look through and sign the paperwork; the most important part being the consent form giving him permission to use the footage we'd just filmed. "You don't want some of the viewers trying to track you down," he advised me. The footage he'd shot, a little earlier, playing through on his laptop once more.

I felt comfortable with Richard. He seemed to genuinely care about the people he worked with. All my worries and stresses about what may have been asked of me, in this industry, were appeased the moment he introduced himself. He'd told me to relax and that nothing would be asked of me that I wasn't comfortable with. He went through the list I'd compiled, with the agent, double-checking the boxes the agent and I had ticked. It was then he suggested we started with something relatively straight forward; in this instance the act of giving someone a blow-job. He'd gone on to explain that he found it the best way of seeing exactly how comfortable a girl was going to be on camera. After all - unless you're mentally prepared - it's not as easy as it sounds; to suck someone off whilst another person films. Certainly most of my friends deemed a blow job to be a more intimate act compared to the act of letting a man fuck you. It also showed that, if need be, you were more than capable of taking charge of the situation. Nine films out of ten, according to Richard, started with the act of giving head. The girl would kiss the man, he'd grope her as she worked her way down to his testicles and then she'd start to suck him off. A few minutes later she'd move around to enable the man the opportunity to lap at her pussy as she continues to suck him off. That was about six minutes of film. Then she'd move down and get into the reverse cowgirl position, squatting down on the man, in order to fuck him. A few more minutes of film - and then the man would take charge. The only major difference in the films was the 'plot' at the beginning to get the proceedings started, the dialogue spoken throughout (depending on the type of scene it was) - at least, that's the way 'vanilla' porn films seemed to go.

Richard had explained the fetish scene (60% of his films were in this market) and then all rules were thrown out of the window. The films may start off with a single man getting blown by a girl but - chances are - a second man wouldn't be far behind. And then it's all about double penetration, sucking them both off, getting facially covered in hot sperm. These films may have involved outfits of some description, nurses and latex being two of the popular film choices, they may have involved bondage (either the girl tied or the man tied)...It was at that point Richard stopped and summed it all up with, "There's something for everyone in this market, however weird something may seem - rest assured someone is out there whacking off to it."

I'd asked him what the strangest film he had ever made had featured. I wasn't curious to see the darkest of fetishes available but more curious to see what I could, potentially, have been asked to do.

"Some guy lying on his back," he'd said with a grimace, "whilst two girls took it in turns to shit over him whilst he tugged himself off. You could almost hear me and the camera-guy heaving off shot. Absolutely disgusting. But that is going back a couple of years when that sort of video was all the rage online. Not for me. I think I prefer shooting the more vanilla of porn films, you know?"

By 'vanilla' he apparently meant films which didn't show any hint of fetishism. They were just a couple of regular (model-like) actors and actresses having sex in whatever way they were instructed.

"And that film sold well?" I had asked him referring to the fetish video he'd described.

"You bet. Like I said, something for everyone. Really grim though, the guy.." he had started to laugh, "the guy ejaculated over himself and started wiping it further around his body with the scat. Next thing, and I swear I didn't ask them to, the girls just started lapping it off him as though it were just chocolate." He paused. "I don't think I ate for a week after that."

The current conversation we were having was more fixated with my name choice. For the sake of my privacy, and avoiding some potential stalkers, he was insisting I went with a made-up name. Even if I didn't do anything other than this one film, and no stalkers hunted me down, it still meant it would be harder for my mum and dad to discover what I'd become.

"I'm not sure," I told him. Up until this point I hadn't given it any consideration whatsoever. It's not as though my agent had warned me. Maybe he had known the producer would help me out with it? Maybe he wasn't as concerned with my wellbeing as this man was.

"Well you can keep the first name but it might be an idea to shorten it a bit," he suggested.

"Vicky?"

"Yeah. And the surname - think Bond girls…"

"I'm sorry?"

"You know - Pussy Galore…The innuendos are great and work in your favour for getting people to remember you. You need something off the wall, something that will stand out and just catch on, you know?" He was watching my on screen performance when he suddenly clicked his fingers as an idea hatched in his head, "Blows. Vicky Blows."

I couldn't help but laugh. Not sure whether out of embarrassment. With what was going on, on screen in front of us, and the name - it was a little cringe-worthy. Cringe-worthy but exciting.

"What do you think?" he asked.

"I like it," it wasn't as though I had any better suggestions to put forward.

Richard smiled as he scribbled the name on top of the forms he'd just got me to sign. I'm not sure whether it was a necessary procedure or whether he did it so he wouldn't forget.

"And I believe this is yours," he said, reaching into his jacket pocket and pulling out an envelope. He handed it to me. It wasn't sealed and I could see a wad of notes contained within. I tried to hide my pleasure at seeing the amount of money. In my mind I'd already spent it on clearing some of the mounting money troubles I was experiencing. Why did I hide the fact I was happy to see the cash? I didn't want to appear desperate. I didn't want him thinking I could be purchased for less than the going rate for girls such as myself. He paused a moment as he gave me another once over; a casual glance which made me feel nervous for the first time since being with him.

"What is it?" I asked.

"Your performance was a little," he hesitated and fell silent a moment.

I squirmed in my chair. He'd been making all the right noises whilst watching the film back and Darren seemed happy enough with my performance.

"We need people to believe you want the sex when they watch the films. You need to project their ideal fantasy woman," Richard explained.

"And what is their ideal fantasy woman?" It was fair enough him telling me that I needed to project this image of a wanton sex maniac but a few more pointers would have been nice. After all - how do you know what the people are looking for when they tune in? Surely each person would be looking for something different - especially given the wide range of adult videos available.

"Whatever I tell you it is when directing. Whatever the script tells you it is."

"I'm not sure I understand," I said - feeling a little foolish.

"The role requires you to act like a nervous school girl? Act like a nervous school girl. Be timid, go with the flow as the male takes the lead. We need you to be dominant? Step it up a gear. Basically the viewer wants you to be whatever the script - for want of a better word - is asking of you."

"But everyone has different tastes, how do I know I'm getting it right?"

"It's because everyone has different tastes that you know you're doing it right. If people pick up the film - it's because they're drawn to the style of movie advertised on the sleeve; school girl, nurse, secretary, boss...The list is endless. You just need to become the character we ask you to become. It's simple."

"You asked me to suck him off. I sucked him off."

"You sucked him off as though he were your boyfriend. It's different to sex in the porn industry. You need to make noises, do more deep throat action - can you even do that? - more eye contact, when catching your breath - talk dirty to him, ask if he likes you wanking his massive manhood...When a camera is rolling never act like it's a regular partner. Step it up a gear. People don't want to see boyfriend / girlfriend sex in any pornography they watch. They want to see a stallion going hard at it with a nymphomaniac slut. The Porn Star Experience."

"You said I did a good job?"

"And you did - your technique obviously worked on the sexual side of things - but your performance needs to be fine tuned." He paused a moment, "Usually I wouldn't see a girl such as yourself again, not after a performance like that, but - I don't know - there's something about you...I can't put my finger on it and I've been trying since the camera started rolling...There's something about you which makes me want to give you another shot."

"What?" my brain was starting to hurt. One minute he was happy with my performance and the next he wasn't and then he was offering me a shot.

* * * * *

"Oh my God, I'm sorry!" I hurried back over to where Harry was still restrained to the pillar, having checked that the camera was still recording our action (it was). "I'm sorry," I repeated, "I don't know what I'm doing...Please...I just haven't been myself recently. Things have gone a little...I've gone a little...crazy."

He seemed to breathe a sigh of relief, "Look just let me out of here and we'll forget the whole thing. Okay? We'll go our separate ways and never speak to each other again." He seemed relieved.

"Okay. Thank you. Jesus...I just don't know what came over me. I just..."

"Just let me out. It's fine."

"Hang on..." I undid the front zipper on my latex catsuit and revealed a small padlock key hanging from a necklace around my neck. I lifted it over my head and disappeared around the back of the pillar to where the locks were. I fiddled with them for a moment - making them rattle against the chains and then stopped. I couldn't keep it up any longer and started to laugh.

"What are you doing?" he asked. "Just let me out."

I walked back around to the front of the pillar and waved the small key in front of his face, with a smile on my face. Before he had a chance to say anything I threw it across the warehouse floor. It landed somewhere in the corner; immediately lost to plain vision.

"Oops," I laughed.

"What the fuck are you doing?" he barked.

I smiled at him again and told him, "I'm proving how far my acting has come since Richard took me under his wing. At this particular moment, your fantasy girl was a girl who'd let you out of your restraints. For a brief moment - you believed that girl was me. See - I had you fooled. Richard would be proud. I've come a long way."

"You're fucking crazy."

"If I am - it's because you made me so."

* * * * *

Richard looked me in the eye, "I'm saying - how'd you like the opportunity to shoot another scene with us?"

I jumped at the chance and blurted out, "Yes!"

"Just remember - when the camera rolls you're no longer you. You're a living, breathing, fucking fantasy portraying whatever role we ask of you. Once you get that...Once you get that I think you'll go far."

"Thank you! Thank you for the opportunity. And the advice. I really do appreciate it." I wasn't sure whether I was supposed to hug him to show my gratitude or simply shake hands but I ended up doing neither. He just smiled at me.

"Some of us are meeting for dinner tonight - a few actors and actresses, the usual motley crew I go with - I think it would be a good idea if you came with me. Meet some of the people you'll potentially be working with. What do you say?"

"I'd love to, thank you."

He smiled again, "It's a date. I'll have a car come pick you up about eight," he said.

A date? A business date? A proper date? I felt a tingle of anticipation run through my body. A business date. It had to be a business date. He didn't know me. Why would he call it a normal date? He meets girls - pretty girls - every day. Why'd he want to have a date with me?

"You okay?" he asked.

"Yeah, I'm good, thanks." I hesitated. Part of me wondered whether I should ask him to clarify what he meant - and I nearly did - but then I realised it would just be stupid to do so. If anything if might push him away from even wanting to help me. "Well, thank you for today, I guess we're done for now then?"

"Yes," he smiled, "thank you for everything today."

"No. It was my pleasure." He extended his hand and we shook, like professionals.

Until dinner then.

DINNER BETWEEN FRIENDS

"I was a nervous wreck when I walked into the restaurant," I called over to Harry. I was standing by a work-bench at the side of the warehouse. Not sure what the bench was usually used for but today it was a catering bench. Not the most hygienic of work spaces but it'll do. I was making us some dinner; sandwiches to be precise. We had a long night together and we both needed to keep our strength up. At least I need to keep my strength up and he needs to maintain an erection and he wasn't about to swallow these pills by choice...

Ensuring he couldn't see what I was doing, I crunched the small blue pills into a fine powder using the edge of the mug he was about to be drinking from. When they were nothing but a powder I scraped it into the very same mug. I added hot tea from a thermal flask and gave it a stir. Hopefully this will work.

"If anything I think I might have been more nervous about going to the dinner than I was going to the initial meeting. I don't know. I guess I felt as though they'd all be judging me. Worse yet - I thought they might not like the idea that

Richard was contemplating using me as an actress. They might have thought of me as competition, or something..."

"Why would they look at you as competition?" Harry spat. "You're nothing. They would have looked at you and seen that straight away. You're a nothing. Ugly even. Blonde hair - dyed of course. Your breasts are small and your tummy...Not as flat as it could be. No girl, in the industry or not, would think of you as competition. If anything - they'd feel sorry for you. We all felt sorry for you...My crew. My actors...We pitied you."

"Was that before or after you did what you did to me?" I knew what he was doing. Trying to get me angry, trying to get a rise out of me. But there was nothing he could do. Nothing that could top what they'd done to me that night anyway.

"Before...... You should have thanked us for what we did for you. You know how many hits that film had? We made you a star. Overnight. We turned you into a someone."

"You destroyed me. You didn't make me. You killed me." I felt myself start to get angry and tried my best to calm down. I shook it from my system. Don't get angry. Don't get hasty and bring the evening to a head already. Not yet. I want to go all night. I want us to go all night. I looked back down to the drink resting on the bench. It looked perfect. Like a normal tea. I gave it another stir - just to be sure. Satisfied I walked back over to where Harry was bound; his plate of sandwiches in one hand and his tea in the other. Nothing for me until I was happy he'd consumed all I had to offer.

"Ham and cucumber," I told him after I had put the cup of tea down. I picked one of the sandwiches up and held it to his mouth. He didn't eat. That's fine. Didn't think he would. Not without some persuasion anyway. I put the plate on the floor and held the sandwich back to his mouth. He still refused to open up to take a bite. I smiled and grabbed his testicles with my spare hand. A hard squeeze and he yelped out in pain. As soon as he opened his mouth, I took the opportunity to ram the sandwich in. "You can do this the easy way or the painful way," I told him, "I don't actually mind which but knowing what I've lined up for you - later - you may want to take the opportunity to have a break from the pain."

He bit down on the sandwich, taking a chunk off, and I pulled the remainder away - giving him the space to chew it of his own accord.

"Good pet!"

I released his testicles. He swallowed his mouthful and I force fed him another. No resistance this time. I like it that he learns his lessons so quickly. When he finished his half of sandwich, I reached down to the cup of tea and lifted it from the floor. I put it to his mouth and held it there carefully to allow him the opportunity to take a sip. Don't want to burn him. Don't want to spill any. Need him to drink all of this - every single drop. Need that erection.

"If you want to talk," he suggested, "get me down from here and we'll talk."

"You know that wouldn't work." I held the cup back to his mouth.

"This is stupid. You're going to have to let me go at some point," he said.

I smiled. He reminded me of where I had got to with my story. The path which enabled us to meet. I continued, "Apparently the meal wasn't just a social event. It was a chance for the staff to say goodbye to one of their own..."

* * * * *

Richard had raised his glass in the air - standing at the head of the long table in the corner of the restaurant - and was halfway through a speech. I was sitting a few seats away, towards the centre of the table. On one side of me was Darren and on the other was a pretty brunette whose name I hadn't yet been told. Knowing what Darren and I had done earlier in the day I felt a little awkward. I know it was just a job - well, an audition - but, even so, I had had the man's penis in my mouth and his cum dribbling down my chin. It was like sitting next to an ex-boyfriend.

"And we wish you nothing but the greatest success in your new role," he finished. The group cheered - their cheers aimed towards the woman sitting next to Richard. Her name was Jodie and she had been one of his main girls for (apparently) many a film. There wasn't much she wouldn't do but now her time had come. By choice, she was moving on to pastures greener - in this instance she was moving into underwear design. According to Darren it wasn't uncommon

42

for women to move into that line of work when they felt as though they had had enough of the porn industry. I guess - after years of wearing underwear on set - they believed they had ideas of what would be comfier for women. Looking at her, she still looked good though. She could have continued making films and she would have still been highly sought after. I wanted to ask her why she had chosen to move on now - and not later - but, being the new girl on the scene, I guessed she'd probably not really want to go into it with me; no doubt worried I'd be judging her decision, not that I would. After all, I was the woman who'd just decided to get into the adult film industry.

Richard didn't take his seat. He stayed standing until the group fell silent again, to hear what else he had to say, "And as one lady leaves us - another joins us." I felt my heart skip a beat as all eyes turned to me. It didn't matter what the situation was or whether it was between friends or strangers, I never did like being the centre of attention. People often found that funny about me, considering I always wanted to be an actress, but I used to tell them that - being an actress meant I didn't have to be me. I could be someone else. And nine times out of ten I'd be in front of a camera as opposed to a large group of people. I felt myself blush as I thanked Richard for the welcome. "Shot her first scene with us today!" Richard continued.

Darren butted in, with a smile on his face, "And very enjoyable it was too." The group laughed. Not sure I can go any redder. I just wanted to hide under the table until the moment had passed. On the plus side though, everyone

seemed happy. They were smiling at me, they had their
glasses raised and they genuinely seemed happy to welcome
me onboard.

* * * * *

Harry started to laugh, "They were actors," he hissed. "You
think they were happy to see you? You think they wanted
you there? All those people sitting around the table
pretending to be friends with each other. They would always
be in competition with each other and someone is always
flavour of the month, taking all the roles for themselves. You
think any of the girls there would have wanted you to
become part of that little 'family'? You're naive. A fucking
idiot."

I was a little startled by Harry's sudden outburst but tried not
to show it. Of course he's going to try and say things to catch
me off guard, to distract me from what I am trying to do -
anything to try and save himself. I had known this before I
had put the plan into action. I knew he'd try it. I just need to
block it from my mind. Just need to shun it. He laughed,
"How do you think I find girls like you?" he continued. "You
really think I get to people like you through your agents?
Come on - they wouldn't work with me. They wouldn't send
people my way for work, no matter how much money I
offered."

"What?" Panic rushed over me. I had presumed that my
agent had given Harry my number. I had presumed it was
because of him that I had ended up on that shoot. I blamed
him. I took out my initial anger on him; my agent.

"You think I wouldn't have been shut down already had I gone through the proper channels already? We would have been out of business before our first film had even been released."

"Of course you went through my agent - how else would you have got my number?" I asked, a sinking feeling in the pit of my gut made me feel as though I wanted to vomit at his feet. I held it in and dismissed it; wouldn't give him the satisfaction.

"One of your newfound girlfriends in your - what did you call it - 'happy family' passed on your details to me. They wanted you off the scene before you'd even got on the scene to take work from them," he laughed. "It's how I get all of my girls. Same thing every time. Your numbers are passed onto us by people who'd sooner you vanished from the scene…"

* * * * *

All the smiles around the table, pointing at me, and I couldn't help but notice the one person who looked angry, Jodie. The lady who was leaving the industry to follow her own passions. She was staring at me and just looked pissed. I couldn't help but feel she was angry because Richard had turned everyone's attention towards me and away from her on her 'goodbye meal'. A night which should have been used celebrating her, as a person, and wishing her success in the future had entirely been turned away from her. But that wasn't my fault. I didn't have a say. Surely she could have seen by my flushed cheeks that I'd have rather not been mentioned at all - other than a quick introduction (maybe one on one) just so I could try and learn their names. Not this though. This was just awkward. I smiled at her hoping my own smile would cause the same from her but it didn't. She simply turned her attention back to Richard who was still addressing me with his good luck speech and how excited he was to have me at their table. Someone please just shoot me and put me out of my misery now. So embarrassing.

* * * * *

"Jodie."

Harry laughed, "You just told me the meal was like a leaving do for her. According to you she was going to go and follow other pursuits. If that was the case - why would she want you away from the scene? Maybe if you were looking at setting up a lingerie range, or something, she may have wanted you gone but...Come on. She was out of the game. You weren't competition for her."

"She was the only one who didn't seem pleased to see me at the table," I defended my accusation.

"Here's this man singing your praises in front of everyone when really he should have been spending the night singing hers. You're an idiot. A fucking idiot. You know that, right? It wasn't this Jodie girl and it wasn't your agent..." He started to laugh - no doubt he'd seen the panic on my face. "What have you done?" he asked, a smile on his face.

I stepped away from him and returned to the work-bench where my own sandwich and (drug-free) drink were waiting. I kept my back to Harry so he couldn't see my face.

What had I done?

AN AGENT FIRED

I had numerous missed calls from my agent. I knew why he was calling. I knew why they were all calling. They wanted to find me. They wanted to track me down so they could finish what they started (and caught on film) before I had the time to go to the police to tell them what had happened. They wouldn't find me here; not at my parents' house.

Mum and dad instinctively knew something was wrong. The bruises which had been visible were healed now and the ones on my body, which hadn't entirely healed, were hidden from their sight with jeans and long sleeved tops. They didn't ask what the matter was though. I'd been raised in a family where problems weren't discussed unless the one experiencing the issue was the one to bring it up; and I wasn't about to do that. Even if I had wanted to - where would I have begun? How much would I have had to tell them? They didn't know what I'd been doing for the last few months and, hopefully, they'd never get to know. It was to be my dirty little secret - not that I felt embarrassed about it. Initially I had been apprehensive about becoming that sort of actress but those apprehensions had soon disappeared the more roles I had taken on and the more familiar I had become with the way the industry worked. Just because I was at ease with it though didn't mean the rest of 'normal' society would have been. They'd have labelled me (incorrectly) with such titles as 'prostitute', 'slut', 'tramp' and 'whore'. All mum and dad had said was that if I wanted to talk I knew where they were.

It broke my heart not being able to tell them what had happened. I felt as though I needed to get it off my chest but knew that I couldn't; unless I lied about the circumstances surrounding the events and I didn't want to lie. Not anymore.

Even though I was safe with my parents and away from the city, I felt as though I were trapped. I couldn't leave the house for fear of them finding me and I couldn't stop from playing back the events which had occurred; my mind seemingly torturing me by not letting me forget and constantly questioning how it had come to be. Each time the latter question was answered with the same conclusion; it had come to be because of him. My agent. I guessed he must have been offered a vast amount of money, probably the money which had initially been discussed as my own payment. The way the evening had gone, they had never had any intention of paying me so it would have been fitting that he'd get it. The only thing I couldn't understand, or contemplate, was why he'd have accepted it. Surely he would have earned more by keeping me alive. I had become a name within the industry with more and more producers stepping forward to work with me. Surely, with his commission, we could have both gone on to make some decent money? The only answer I could come up with was the possibility of his greed getting hung up on the fact that this payment, the most I'd ever been offered, was upfront. He didn't have to wait. He didn't have to hawk me around to the producers. He just had to make me sign on the dotted line and then - done - that was it. The money would be his just as soon as they'd finished with me.

The thought of his betrayal made me feel physically sick. More so when I wondered how many other women he'd led down this darker path. How many other girls had gone where I had ventured to but not been so lucky? And once those thoughts dissipated from my mind - all I could think about was hurting him. Not just him. All of them. Everyone who'd been involved in the deal and the production. I wanted them to suffer as much as I had. Worse.

The nights were filled with broken dreams; nightmares where I relived the scene again and again. Every time I woke up, and then finally drifted off back to sleep, the dream seemed to pick up from where it was initially left. There was no escape from it. Nothing I could do to stop it from playing out in my subconscious. And every time I relived the moments, I always felt the pain and suffering that I'd been forced to endure. If anything, in this dream state, it seemed to be magnified.

Days and nights became blurred into one. I can't remember how often mum and dad came into the room to check up on me - to see if I wanted anything. Both of them were aware I hadn't been eating properly since coming home that night. I just wasn't hungry. The sickness in my stomach refusing to leave me. I felt unsettled. Hardly surprising that I had started to feel bad a few weeks later. Without eating properly my body was starting to ache. Felt run down.

* * * * *

"What did you do to your agent?" Harry was still laughing; his laughter pulled me from my thoughts. He knew what I'd done to my agent. He'd received the same treatment as the others. He received what I felt he deserved. What I wrongly believed he deserved. There's that sickness in my stomach again. "Oh man," Harry continued to laugh, "this is too good. You did, didn't you?" Don't say it. Please don't say it. "This is fucking priceless." He tried to stop laughing, "Tell me I'm wrong. Tell me you didn't..." He paused, waiting for me to deny it but I couldn't. He knew it and I knew it. "You killed him."

I hurried over to the pillar and spat in his face, my anger getting the better of me, "Fuck you!" I hissed. Even with my spit running down his face he continued to laugh at me.

"You killed an innocent man. Look at you thinking you're on some sort of mission of justice. A fucked up crime-fighter bringing justice to the evils of the world," he was teasing me, "yet look what you've gone and done. You're no better than me. No, scratch that, you're worse than me. I've never killed anyone." He continued, "So how does this work? You can't stand here preaching to me about the rights and wrongs of the world when you're no better than me - when you're worse..."

51

"Shut the fuck up!" I reached into the bag and pulled out a hammer. I put it against the side of his head; a threat to show him how easy it would have been to swing at his skull.

"Just do it!" he shouted. "If you're going to do it, fucking do it! Put me out of my misery."

I pulled the hammer away. Clever. He'd nearly got me. Or rather, my temper had nearly got the better of me.

"You can't do it, can you? You're fucking pathetic."

I shook my head, "You think it's going to be that easy? I don't think so." I dropped the hammer to the floor where it landed with a thud - a thud which echoed around the large room. "I see what you're trying to do and I understand why you're doing it but...we have the whole night together, baby, and..." I pointed to the camera, "...people are going to want us to put a show on for them. We have much to talk about yet and we have much to do."

"LET ME OUT OF HERE!" he screamed at me - rattling the chains again.

I smiled sweetly and moved closer until my mouth was next to his ear. I gently blew with every word I whispered, "Want to know how I killed my agent?" I purred. It bothered me that I'd killed someone who didn't have anything to do with what had happened but I couldn't let that show. Not again. I needed him to believe I was fine with taking a life.

* * * * *

PORN

My agent, Frank, opened the door to his apartment and peered down the corridor.

"Anyone there?" he asked.

I was there. Not that I replied to him. I stayed quiet. Tucked against the door to his neighbour's apartment so I wouldn't be seen. I had knocked on my manager's door and retreated back to where I couldn't be seen.

"You're not funny!" he called out.

I wasn't trying to be funny. I was trying to get him out of his apartment. I wanted him to walk down the length of the corridor of apartment doors, right up to the end of the corridor so he could look down the next which lead the way to the lifts and stairs. That was why I hid outside this apartment. There was nowhere for anyone to go if they ran this way so little point in Frank coming this way.

"Fuck off!" he called out as he stepped back into his apartment.

Damn. Didn't come out. Didn't venture to the end of the corridor in the effort to catch any possible pranksters. I waited, patiently. There was little point in knocking now. Not with him so close to the door. I know he'd be waiting for another knock (my fourth). I know he'd be trying to catch me out. I had to be patient. I had to wait for him to go and make himself comfortable again. I counted away the minutes in my head and waited for five of them to pass. That should do it. That should have given him enough time to go back to doing whatever he was doing in there. I left my rucksack on the floor, next to the door where I'd been waiting, and made my back to the next door. Again, just as I had done on the previous occasions, I hit the door with my clenched fist. Three hits and I hurried back to my hiding spot and waited.

The door opened again. Frank didn't call out but I could still hear that he was seething at the thought of someone pranking him. And then I heard what I was waiting for; footsteps. I carefully peered around the corner and noticed he was walking away - towards the corridor with the lifts. I seized my opportunity and grabbed my bag from the floor before darting into his apartment.

The television was on, a dirty movie. Not just any dirty film but one of my earlier films. I watched, for just a second, and instantly remembered filming the scene. One of the many school-girl roles I'd played. It was me and another lady. In the scene we took our teacher by surprise during a late, after-school detention. He was getting masterful with us when we started to masturbate in front of him. He just sat there, for a few minutes of footage, rubbing his crotch through his trousers as he watched as we fingered ourselves (and each other). After the initial scene-setting minutes, we made our way to him. We got on our knees and freed his pulsing erection from his trousers. I can't remember the lines we had to say. Regardless, it ended with us both going down on him; licking and sucking on his shaft whilst he moaned and pushed down (from time to time) on our heads, causing us to occasionally gag as he penetrated our throats. The apartment door shut and brought me back to the present. I hid behind the living room door before he saw me. Just in time too. Seconds later he walked into the room and took his seat in front of the television. I peered out from my hiding place and watched as he quickly stood up; long enough to pull his trousers down. Bare-assed, he sat back down. Seconds later and I could hear exactly what he was doing with his hand; the sound of skin on skin. Rubbing. At this rate he wouldn't even make it past the initial minutes - the tamer opening scene. I nearly laughed.

I slammed the door and he jumped up, still with his cock in his hand. He face instantly red.

I was smiling at him.

"What the fuck are you doing here?" he asked. Panic on his face. Hardly surprising considering he'd been caught with his pants down. He pulled them up.

"Don't."

"What?"

"Don't. Never really saw you like that before but - wow - impressive."

Despite my instruction to leave his pants down, he pulled them up.

* * * * *

"He wasn't the only man I'd seen standing in front of me with a surprise erection," I purred into Harry's ear. My hand roamed downwards, to his genitals. The viagra was working and his cock was pulsing under my touch. Harry sighed, enjoying the feeling of my touch once more.

* * * * *

"You're a fan?" I asked Frank.

He turned to the television and realised he'd been busted watching one of my movies - not just any dirty movie. Not that either scenario was less embarrassing than the other.

"Where have you been?" he stuttered. "I've been trying to call you."

I stayed by the door, unsure as to how he was going to react at me being in his apartment. Clearly he wasn't expecting to see me again. Clearly, after sending me to the film shoot, he didn't want to see me again. Cock in hand or not, potentially he was dangerous.

"I know. I was taking some time for myself. Collecting my thoughts."

"I've been trying to find you," he said.

"I bet."

He wasn't making a move towards me, or doing anything to defend himself. I'm not sure why but this surprised me. I thought he may have tried to finish what they had started but here he was - standing in front of me - pretending as though everything was okay between us. Well...Everything was okay other than the fact I'd caught him masturbating to one of my films.

"Can I get you a drink?" he asked.

I shook my head.

"So - what brings you here?" he continued.

I took a step closer to him. He still didn't make any effort to move from where he was seemingly rooted to the spot.

"You."

"I beg your pardon?"

"I missed you. Wanted to see you."

His face reddened again.

"Well, I've missed you too," he stuttered again. "So many jobs have been coming in for you. Had to tell people you were on a holiday. If you want, I can grab my laptop and we can go through them now."

I shook my head.

"Not here for business."

"No?"

"No."

He paused, "I don't understand - why are you here?"

"Pleasure."

"What?"

I walked over to him. Before he had a chance to move away I reached down and cupped his testicles. His cock was still erect. A typical man. They forget all common sense, leave it all behind, when there's a pretty girl in front of them. More so when said pretty girl has a hold of their cock.

"Why'd you put it away?" I asked.

He hesitated, "I wasn't expecting company."

"No need to stop what you were doing," I leaned around him and nodded towards the television, "it's getting hotter."

He turned to the screen where the two girls were now taking it in turn to suck on their teacher's cock.

* * * * *

"He seemed to have a harder time taking his eyes off the screen this time," I purred as I started stroking Harry's cock harder and faster - a grip I'd learned most men were unable to resist. "I told him to sit down," I continued, "and pushed him back onto his seat. I told him to keep watching the television as I mirrored my character's actions on screen; taking him into my mouth and sucking him, licking him, nibbling him.."

I lowered myself to my knees. Harry tried to move away from me - no doubt remembering the feeling of my teeth against his shaft - but I held him in place before wrapping my lips around his dick. I started sucking and licking, keeping the fast hand movement going on the lower end of the shaft. Harry's breathing changed - just as Frank's had.

* * * * *

On screen my character positioned herself until she was straddling her teacher's lap. Gently she lowered her sopping cunt onto his penis which slid in easily. I watched, for a minute, as I continued to wank the cock in my hand. I looked up at Frank. His eyes were fixed on the screen. I stood up, still wanking him with my left hand, and pulled my knickers down - from under my skirt - with my right hand. I stepped out of them and mirrored the position demonstrated on screen.

"What are you doing?" he asked.

"Ssh! I've wanted this for so long," he slid into me easily. The lubrication I had squirted into myself earlier still doing its job of keeping me moist enough to take the sting off. I faked a moan of pleasure as Frank sighed with one of genuine satisfaction. "How's that?" I asked.

"Amazing."

I smiled.

* * * * *

The latex catsuit I was wearing had a zipper which ran the length of the under-carriage. It allowed access to either orifice without the need to remove the suit. I slid the zip from front to back freeing either option for Harry. I turned around and bent over in front of him. Slowly I backed into him - using my hand to guide his penis into my pussy. Once inside I started rocking backwards and forwards with a steady rhythm.

"Frank's breathing sounded like yours does now," I sighed as I rocked back and forwards on the erection, "...The feeling of my cunt, the wetness, the tightness..."

The fact Harry wasn't telling me to stop just proved my point about how pathetic men were (are) when presented with a willing sexual partner. I'll let him enjoy it for now. Just as I'll let myself enjoy it too. Not because of the sexual feeling. But because I know what it means for Harry. That in itself is enough to get me on the verge of climaxing; not that I'll go all the way with him. Not yet anyway.

* * * * *

"I've wanted this from the moment you came into my office," he sighed.

"Me too," I lied. "From the moment I first met you I just wanted to fuck you. I wanted to fuck your brains out. Wanted you inside me. Deep inside. Filling me. Fucking me." The dirtier I spoke the more he sighed. Looking at his face, he didn't know where to look, torn between watching me on the television - rimming the other school girl whilst teacher fucked me hard from behind, or watching me fuck him for real. I increased the pace, helped by his hands around my buttocks rocking me. His breathing quickening further. I knew it wouldn't be much longer. I knew he was on the verge of ejaculating. His face contorted as he took a deep breath in and then...His whole body twitched. I slowed my rocking down to a gentler pace as he shot his load into my pussy. I smiled.

"Well," he breathed heavily, "that was unexpected." He started to laugh. As did I but not for the same reason. We weren't sharing a joke. I had my own joke. I leaned forward and french kissed him - his hands still on my arse cheeks. I pulled them off and climbed from his now-shrinking penis, letting a little semen dribble out of my cunt and onto his lap. He looked down to the mess we'd made, "Completely creamed me," he laughed. I smiled at him as I pulled my underwear back up.

* * * * *

I moved forward and let Harry slide out of me. His erection still standing proudly thanks to the viagra; not that I think he'd have had trouble maintaining an erection at this point in our relationship.

"And then I left the apartment. Went back to a new flat I'd moved into since our last encounter; somewhere you didn't know about. Somewhere you wouldn't find me."

"You said you killed him," Harry was catching his breath; still turned on from our encounter.

"It's what I said to him, as I left, that killed him." It's what I said after I kissed him again. I moved forward and grabbed Harry by his hair and forced my tongue into his mouth. He didn't fight me, he went along with it, clearly enjoying himself. Enjoy it whilst you can. Things are about to change. I pulled away. "I whispered to him," I said as I moved to Harry's ear once more, "...Welcome to the HIV club."

I moved back and enjoyed the horror on Harry's face. I couldn't help but laugh, Frank had had a similar expression.

* * * * *

"What?" Frank stuttered.

"Don't be surprised, honey, you did this to me. You and your dirty fucking friends."

"What?" he stuttered again.

"Now whenever you have sex, whenever you start to feel a little under the weather...You can think of me, you can think of what I've done to you and why." I gave him a wink and walked from the apartment before he had the chance to say anything else. Just as my life was over, so was his.

* * * * *

"Don't worry," I told Harry. "You won't live long enough to have it ruin your life. You won't even live long enough to know if - me fucking you - even passed it on to you. You won't survive the night but I somehow don't think you'll be worrying about that yet. I think, despite knowing you'll be dead today, you'll be more worried about the infection possibly flowing through your bloodstream."

Harry was clearly upset, "Why are you doing this to me?" he asked again - as though it hadn't been discussed a million times before.

"Because you did this to me. Your actor - the man you made..." I stopped myself, "I wasn't ready to talk about that yet. I wasn't at that point of the story yet. I continued, "...he was HIV positive and now - thanks to you - so am I. And there's a good chance you are too, just as there's a strong possibility Frank, my agent, is as well."

Harry started to cry; this surprised me.

"I didn't know!" he wept. "I didn't know!"

"Okay, calm down. No sense getting upset yet. We have a long night ahead of us. In fact, what say we have a break?"

He didn't answer me. He didn't even acknowledge me. He just kept repeating again and again how he hadn't known that his main actor had been HIV positive. Whether he knew or not - it didn't matter. The fact was - he'd told him to fuck me bareback despite knowing I didn't want that. I told him - I was going to do to him as he did to me. That was the first stage. He got what he deserved. And - as I had told him - it's not as though he'd have to live with the consequences of our sexual liaison. Not like I would. Not point reiterating the point though; clearly he's distressed. A time out will do us both some good. He just needs a little sleep and I have just

MATT SHAW

the thing to send him off...

A TIME OUT

I walked over to the camera and checked that it was still recording while Harry tried to get his emotions under control. It was still recording. Good. I stopped it for a moment and pressed the rewind button on the side of the view-finder. I couldn't help but smile as I watched our antics back on screen. Looks like I'd caught everything. Satisfied, I fast forwarded through to the end of the filmed footage and hit the record button again. I zipped the lower section of the cat-suit up again and walked back over to Harry. He was still snivelling but had managed to calm down some, at least.

"What's the matter?" I asked. "Did you not even enjoy the sex?"

He didn't answer me. Was he really giving me the silent treatment? I laughed and picked the hammer up.

"Look at this erection," I said. I gripped it in my spare hand. "Still standing proud despite the news I've most likely infected you with HIV. Is now a good time to tell you about the drink you had? Yeah - about that - sorry...laced with viagra. This thing isn't going down for hours yet. At least I don't think it will be. Not quite sure what this is going to do,"

I looked at the hammer and back to Harry's face. You could clearly see the panic in his eyes.

"What are you going to do?" he asked.

Oh, now he wants to talk.

"Please - I've suffered enough. Just stop. Please."

I like the sound of his begging. Weird to think that it's making me a little wet. His voice is quiet, I do hope the camera picks it up so I can play it back again and again to my heart's content.

"Condoms are used to protect people from HIV, and other sexually transmitted diseases and infections obviously. But they're also a form of contraception. Like this here hammer..."

"Please," his voice quivered as he looked at the hammer, "...don't."

"Ssh. It's okay. In truth we should have done this before, you know, I slid you inside me. For all we know I might already be infected with your rancid seed. Only takes a drop of pre-cum..." I moved the hammer down and touched the metal head against his own head. He flinched but couldn't go anywhere. He was mine to do with as I pleased. "The important thing is - we didn't forget entirely to do it. And the chances of me being pregnant from that little encounter are probably slim. Still, for the sake of things to come - no pun intended - we take care of this now."

He flinched again as I flipped the hammer around in my hand so that the head was facing upwards towards the warehouse ceiling...towards his testicles. I looked across to the camera, little red-light still flashing; still recording. I looked back to Harry.

"Do you have any children at home?" I asked.

He shook his head.

"And you never will," I laughed.

With that I swung the hammer down and then straight up between his legs as hard and fast as I could. The sound of his testicles being crushed on impact were drowned out by his scream as it bounced off the four walls of the warehouse; an ear-piercing shriek of pain as his complexion immediately turned pale. A second blow, just as hard, and he was unconscious from the shock - just as I had expected, even though I wished he wasn't. I couldn't imagine the pain I had inflicted but still I wished he'd stayed conscious to suffer it for longer. I looked down at the mashed mess of flesh and blood which was once his balls. At least he'll still feel it when he comes round. I put the hammer down on the floor and made my way to the camera. I leaned down so that my face filled the screen.

"To be continued," I told the potential viewers.

I stopped the recording and turned the camera off in order to save the battery power whilst my mind reminded me of the conversation I'd had with Richard. The one which had stated the various strange tastes people had when it came down to their preference for pornographic films. I couldn't help but wonder whether there'd be anyone out there who'd masturbate to this when it was uploaded - a part of them wishing they were in Harry's position. I turned away from the scene momentarily and returned to the work-bench where I'd earlier left my food. Need to eat something. Feel sick I'm so hungry. Not taken my medication today either. Always feel bad when I miss a day; something which happens frequently due to the course of revenge I've taken.

HIV.

My mind drifted back to when I first had learned the news...

* * * * *

I had been feeling unwell for a few weeks now. At first the doctor just believed it to be a type of flu and, because I couldn't shift it myself, prescribed me some antibiotics. I took them religiously until the course was complete, just as the instructions dictated, but ended up going back to the surgery within a few days as I still felt run down. It was on this occasion, when I described what I was feeling, that my doctor asked me back in order to complete some blood tests with one of the nurses; something I did within a few days of our appointment. He hadn't told me what he was looking for. He simply said he wanted to rule some things out. I guess he knew to look for HIV because I'd been upfront with my doctor with regards to my profession. Doctor and patient confidentiality meant I felt as though I could trust him. After all - who'd he tell? No one without risking his job and I'm sure a little gossip wasn't worth that much to him.

Should have known he was concerned the illness was some kind of infection. He was asking about my job and what I'd been doing recently. A few questions in and he stopped beating around the bush and just came out with what he really wanted to ask: Had I recently had unprotected sex?

I remember breaking down before he'd even finished asking the question. For so long I had felt alone. I felt as though there was no one I could talk to. No one that would understand. Of course I told him everything and he suggested we got the police involved but I declined his offer of phoning them on my behalf. I didn't want them turning me into a 'case'. Besides - with what they'd done to me - that night - I couldn't say for definite that the News stations wouldn't have got involved. And once the story of what had happened started to hit the headlines, it wouldn't have been long before mum and dad would have read about it and seen how I'd been paying my bills.

Of course the doctor offered me the opportunity to speak to someone who'd had more experience in dealing with cases such as mine but I declined and the next time we spoke to each other - it was to discuss the blood test results. I was HIV positive.

* * * * *

As the doctor's words echoed through my mind, I wanted to storm across the warehouse floor to where Harry was still unconscious. I wanted to take the hammer from where I'd dropped it and continually hit him with it until he breathed no more. I turned my back on him - out of sight and out of mind theoretically - and took a few deep breaths. I haven't come all this way just to put him out of his misery before I'd really caused him as much pain as I possibly could. I want him to feel every bit of rage I have to dish. He hasn't suffered nearly enough yet.

* * * * *

I moved out of mum and dad's home - out of my old childhood bedroom, a place which seemed so safe - and returned to my own flat. Not for long though. I'd already told the estate agent I wanted to move out. I didn't give them the reasons - the worry that...they'd...come for me here. With the savings in my bank, I moved to another location despite having up until the end of the month to move from the current address. I just wanted to get out of there. Get as far away as I could - as though running away would help me forget what happened or what I'd been left with (for the rest of my life).

The doctor was good. Again, he offered counselling sessions - either in groups or one on one. He told me it was sometimes good to talk to people who were going through the same as me but I didn't listen to his advice; at least I didn't take it onboard. I didn't want people knowing my business. I didn't want to see the looks on their faces when I told them that I was - in my eyes - as good as dead. Of course the doctor told me that, with medication, I could live a long life. It wasn't the death sentence it used to be, but to me it was.

For a while, locked away in my new (rented) accommodation, I even contemplated taking my own life. On more than one occasion I tied the cord, from my dressing gown, around my neck and stood beneath the loft hatch with the end of the cord in my hand. The thought process running through my mind being to climb into the loft and hang myself from the rafter. Once - only once - I even managed to get into the loft with the loose end of the cord tied around the rafter, before bottling it and coming back down again.

Taking my medication daily, as ordered, I was nothing but a mess. I hated myself for what had happened because I put the blame on my own shoulders. It was me who put me into this situation. I was the one who had joined the industry, I was the one who had taken the booking offered, I was the one who...And then something snapped inside me; something which told me I wasn't to blame, I wasn't the cause...I was the victim. I was the victim.

Victim.

I was standing in front of the mirror - cracked in an earlier fit of rage and frustration mixed with fear for what the future could bring - when I snapped. I didn't want to be known as a 'victim'. What they did to me certainly made me one but - no - that's not how I'd die. That's not the mark I'd leave behind. My dark thoughts turned away from the appealing nature of wanting to kill myself and turned to ideas - mostly images - of

wanting to kill them. Not just kill them either. I wanted to
hurt them as they'd hurt me. More so.

* * * * *

I was standing at the work-bench in the warehouse;
remembering how I felt standing in front of the mirror. It was
at that point I'd turned my attentions towards my agent. The
mistake in thinking he was the one'd organised the shoot.

I turned back to Harry. Still unconscious. If it wasn't my agent
- who the hell was it? The job had come through to me via his
email address so it was easy to see how I believed he was to
blame. But…Someone else who had access to his computer. I
wondered whether Harry would tell me - when he woke up. I
doubt t. Scum as he is, scum as all of them are, they seem to
be fairly loyal to each other. Even with the dead in sight.
Unless - of course - he tries to use it as a bargaining chip;
he'll tell me who kick-started the whole thing in exchange for
his freedom. Or maybe he'd ask for a quick death? I'm not
prepared to give him either despite wanting the information.
I thought Harry was the last. I'd hoped he was. I'd saved him
to be; both by choice and the fact he was harder to get on his
own.

Despite knowing the chances of him answering my question
(who'd sent me to him) were slim to none, I had to try. I
walked through to the back room again having earlier seen
something which would be handy for now; a dirty old bucket
half filled with (I presume) rainwater which had leaked from
a hole in the ceiling above it. I lifted it via the white handle
and carefully carried it back through to where he was bound

to the pillar. I placed the bucket down and crossed over to the camera. A flick of the switch and the red light started flashing. Recording. I walked back over to the bucket of dirty water and picked it up with both hands.

"Wake up..." I gave him the opportunity to wake up without the water. He didn't stir. So be it. I swung my arms and the water flew from the bucket and splashed across Harry. He woke with a start - immediately screaming. I wasn't sure whether this was because of the cold water or the pain from his testicles. Truth be told; I didn't care either way.

For a split second his expression showed nothing but confusion. Had the sleep given him the opportunity to escape from the warehouse? Can't have that. He screamed again when he realised where he was. Another scream when the pain kicked in.

"Who set up our film?" I asked him, shouting over his own screams.

He didn't answer me. Not sure he even heard me.

"I said, who set up our film? If it wasn't my agent...Who?"

He started to laugh through his tears. "I'll never tell you."

I smiled at him. "Yes. You will."

I threw the bucket towards the corner of the warehouse. Won't be needing that again. I reached down to the bag of goodies I'd brought with me and pulled it open; revealing the insides to Harry. His eyes widened with fear. The result I was hoping for.

"Do you know how your friend died? We're getting to that part of the story and - if you know - I guess we can skip it?"

I reached into the bag and pulled out a small butt-plug.

"What are you doing?" he wheezed through the pain he was already experiencing.

"You need to loosen it up first. A little. It makes it easier when we put bigger things in. And - trust me - we'll be putting bigger things in." I smiled at him. "Thinking about it, you should be thanking me."

"Just kill me..."

"I will. When I'm ready."

"Please." His eyes were rolling in the back of his head. Maybe I shouldn't have started with his testicles. Maybe I should have started a little gentler? Worked up to things like that. Things which are going to be a distraction to what I have to tell him.

"Don't interrupt me." I paused a moment to collect my thoughts. "Right, where was I...Okay...Your friend...Your leading man...Did you find out how he died? I've been busy...Not sure if the reports made the papers. Having said that, did his death even make the papers? Maybe he's still rotting where I left him?" I started to laugh.

"Fuck you!" Harry wheezed.

I smiled again, "You already have. Remember? And now you're potentially HIV. Your last fuck. Your last wet pussy. A poisonous pussy. One you created. You and your leading man. And it started in the ass." Still didn't answer my original question though.

I reached under Harry's smashed testicles, with the small butt-plug, and round to his anus. He tried to shift position but couldn't. He was mine. The restraints made sure of that. Free of lubrication, I pushed the small toy into his arse. He winced. I smiled at his discomfort but - inside - I couldn't help but wonder who had sent that email. Who'd set me up?

THE MOST REQUESTED GIRL

I filmed a scene, with both Richard and Darren, the day after they'd invited me back. The first scene had been so Richard, the producer, could see what I was like at giving a blow-job. The second scene we'd filmed together had me riding Darren as he sat on the settee he'd been on the day before, when I had him in my mouth.

I'm not sure whether it was Richard's easy laid back manner which put me at ease or the fact my nerves were calmed with the previous day's shoot (and dinner with the rest of his film family) and I didn't care. I just remembered showing up feeling good and ready to go; ready to impress. And I must have impressed him.

A couple of days went past, after the shoot, and I received an email from my agent offering me another job. A different producer. Apparently this producer was acquainted with Richard and had been impressed with footage he'd seen. The job on offer was a girl-on-girl scene. It would be my first liaison with another woman.

The taste of the girl on my tongue, as the director asked me to eat her out, was unusual - I remember that much - but not entirely unpleasant. Would I do this without pay? I'm not sure. Hard to say. The feeling of her fingers stroking inside me - hitting my g-spot with perfect precision, though, as her tongue lapped greedily at my clitoris when we changed position. Would I do this without pay? Definitely.

Another day and another shoot. Still nothing unusual asked of me. I'd heard the stories, from Richard, of what could have been asked and I guessed I was lucky to avoid such requests due to my look. Young and innocent. Doesn't really open the door to the more unusual of demands. I had spent some time, between shoots, watching various videos on the internet - easily found with a search on any of the main sites - all based around darker fetishes. All the girls who appeared in them - they seemed to have a different look to me. Older, for one. Not necessarily unpleasant to look at but...Definitely older. Definitely more...Experienced. Maybe these were the requests which would come my way in years to come if I were to still be in the industry? Would I even still be in this industry in years to come? Perhaps these emails and phone calls offering me jobs - perhaps it's just beginner's luck? Maybe my career will be over within a couple of weeks. A few months and it'll be nothing but distant memories and a slightly loose vagina?

Make the most of the jobs whilst they're coming in.

During these weeks, months, I didn't turn anything down. Whatever the job, I accepted it and worked it like a seasoned pro despite being new to the industry. Some even commented on my professionalism but I just laughed it off.

"New ladies usually need a little more coaching," one had commented.

All that time in drama school, trying to get the necessary experience to become an actress. Had I wasted so many years when - all the time - I could have just gone into this? Saved the tuition fees (which I've yet to pay back)? I simply smiled when someone made a comment and thanked them. Richard once said people keep requesting me because I'm genuinely nice. Apparently you didn't get a lot of that in this industry. Instead, he said, it was saturated with bitchiness and egos. Part of me wondered whether I was being requested because of this or because I was good at my job? Maybe they wanted me just because they knew I'd be easy to work with? No drama on set. I don't know. It also made me question his feelings for me again - just as I had done when he asked me out to that dinner. Was it because I was a business colleague or because he liked me? Maybe both. Not sure. Never know.

I spoke about it - what Richard said - to my manager once. He told me not to question it all the time the jobs were coming in. He warned me that - sometimes - careers in this industry could be short-lived.

"Enjoy it while it lasts," he laughed.

Of course he'd say that. He'd want the cut of my fee for all the jobs that were coming in and - if careers were to be short-lived - he'd want to get as much as he could before my time came to an end. I didn't mind though. That's the way the cookie crumbles and all that. And I said 'yes' to every text

and phone call and email that came in. I never had any
reason to doubt him, or the messages themselves.

I'd played the part of a babysitter a couple of times; once I
seduced the husband of the child I was meant to be looking
after and the other time I had been the one who was
seduced. I'd been seduced by the bored next door neighbour
- the lonely housewife looking for a little fun. Sometimes that
role would be just me and the lady. Other times the role
would be the two of us and then her 'husband' when he
walked in and caught us. He acts surprised, we act shocked
and then - next thing - we're all squirming and writhing
around, sucking and fucking and probing. I'd done the school
girl role a couple of times too. The step-sister is probably the
weirdest role I'd done. I just felt it was a little incestuous. I
had to walk into the room where my step-brother was
wanking himself into my underwear. I had to act shocked,
disgusted even, but then I had to calm down and offer to give
him a helping hand. That film was a POV shoot. POV being
'point of view'. The camera was his eyes watching me as I
tugged him off; letting him ejaculate onto my bared breasts.

I was flattered I was getting all the work. It was nice to be
wanted. Especially after getting neglected as a 'real' actress
for so long. Turned down audition after audition after
audition. There's only so much rejection you can take but
now, here I was, the tables turned - people wanted me. All of
them using my previous films as auditions. I just had to turn
up and do what was asked.

And then THE email came in; the one offering me your job. Well - not quite explaining what you wanted - the email read as though it was a standard job; one of the ones I was used to getting.

* * * * *

I was toying with the plug in Harry's asshole. Gently moving it back and forth, twisting it around ever so slightly. I think - had it not been for the state of his balls - he might have enjoyed the sensation. Most men do yet they'd never admit it. Not the done thing. As it was – because of the pain he was busy hyperventilating and whining like an injured dog.

"Did you compose the email?" I asked him. Looking at the state of him, it was clear I wasn't going to get any sensible answers from him anymore. That's fine. He can just listen. "Not important, I guess. For all I know it could have been done by the person who passed me to you...What's important, though, is what happened next. Our meeting. I think it was two days later, if memory serves me correctly and you'll have to forgive me if I am wrong," I said, "I've been through a lot."

* * * * *

I stepped into the coffee house and stood, a moment, in the doorway as I scanned the various faces sitting at the tables. It was the first time I'd met a director and actor in a public place and I suppose it could have felt strange had it not been for the fact I was told, over a quick phone conversation, that his office was currently being renovated. Who was I to question it? Thankfully two men had stood up and were waving me over to their table in the corner of the room. I smiled and walked over to greet them; hopefully the people I was looking to meet and not just two crazy fans who'd recognised me.

"Harry?" I asked.

Harry, a tall skinny man with dark hair and darker eyes flashed his perfect teeth when he smiled. "That's me," he said, extending his hand. We shook. "And - of course - this is Tom who you'd be working with." Tom and I shook hands too. "Can I get you a drink?" Harry asked.

"Coffee would be lovely," I said - not wishing to appear rude.

Harry nodded and headed towards the counter. I took a seat opposite Tom.

"You know," he said, "I don't think his office will ever be finished."

"I'm sorry?"

"I just think he's addicted to these coffees," he laughed, "seriously - we've been coming here for months. I'm surprised he doesn't have his name plate, taken from his office, hanging on this table instead."

I laughed (more out of politeness).

"Okay watch him. Maybe you could answer something for me," he pointed towards Harry who was ordering a round of coffees.

"What?"

"I'm trying to decide whether it's the coffee he comes here for, or that lady."

The girl behind the counter - the one serving him - was a pretty lady. Probably a couple of years older than me. She had red hair and - I think - green eyes. Her smile just as brilliantly white as Harry's, a slender girl who looked great in the black uniform of the coffee house; no doubt one of those girls who'd make any outfit look good. I watched Harry converse with the woman. She seemed oblivious to the fact he was clearly flirting with her; smiling, leaning into the counter to get closer to her, joking around given the fact she seemed to be laughing with him. I wondered what he was saying - not that it was a long conversation as he was soon heading back to our table. He sat opposite me, next to Tom, still smiling.

"What?" Tom asked.

"Boyfriend," Harry laughed. He took a sip from his coffee in a desperate attempt to hide his embarrassment.

"Ah. Say no more."

I felt as though I were intruding. Our business seemingly less important than trying to score a date with the girl behind the counter. Hardly the most professional of beginnings to what could be a new business relationship. Richard really was a diamond in the rough then.

"So," Harry said, "you got the email."

Way to point out the obvious.

"Yes," I said - not wishing to appear as rude as he was coming across.

"Well it's nothing that out of the ordinary," he said. "Reckon the whole thing will most likely take a couple of days to shoot although," he continued, "that's depending on how well Tom here performs." He looked at Tom and gave him a pat on the shoulder.

"Have I let you down yet?" he asked.

"Always time for a first."

Tom looked at me and smiled, "Doubt it'll be this time."

Little bit of vomit at the back of my throat. I felt like standing up and walking out but - and it's a reason I stayed sitting - I couldn't ignore the money offered in the initial email. More money than I have earned so far. In fact, more money than three of my first films combined. Can't ignore that.

"So what sort of scenes are you thinking?" I asked. I wanted to know if there was a story or a link to the scenes - as present in some films - or whether it was literally a handful of scenes strung together with the two of us going at it.

"Sucking, fucking - nothing out of the ordinary."

"No story?"

"Ah - yes - story. It's a superhero parody. You'll be dressed in a tight latex outfit - you can email me your sizes later and we'll ensure we have one ready for you - and he'll be dressed in, like, a black rubber superhero costume. Like Batman without all the hood and shit. You don't pay this much money for your actor to cover the face. People want to see the expressions when he's going at it, you know."

The film sounded cheesy but it could have been a laugh. It would be nice to get dolled up into something different too. So many films in similar outfits - maybe, with people seeing me in latex, it could open the door for more opportunities?

"It'll be just the two of us?" I asked. I knew there'd be more than Tom and I present. There'd be a camera man, possibly a sound man (unless the camera had it's own microphone), sometimes a photographer to capture some stills for the cover artwork, director (Harry in this instance), make-up (although sometimes the girls were left to do it for themselves) and maybe even a few more people milling around. I just didn't know if we'd be the only people to be appearing on film.

"Just the two of you." Harry said with a smile. "Nice and simple that way."

"And what sort of scenes were you looking to shoot? Specifically?" I asked. So far I couldn't see the justification for the high pay offered. I knew I'd slowly started getting a reputation around the circles but there was something about this deal which made it sound too good to be true.

"Specifically? Well you're going to play the villain. Cunt-woman..."

I looked at him with a raised eyebrow. Was he for real?

"And - basically - he's going to try and capture you. You know, take you to jail...BUT...But...You're going to turn the tables on him and he's going to end up tied to a table. You'll be saying something along the lines of wanting to fuck him for so long..."

Cliche, I thought.

"And then you'll start sucking him. Probably a little face-sitting as you pretend you're going to suffocate him with your cunt - your trademark move for killing people - and then - BANG - you fuck."

I looked at Tom. He was simply grinning as he sat there listening to the 'plot'.

"Vaginal intercourse?" I asked.

"Anal if you're up for it."

It would've have been my first anal scene on tape. My first anal, to be honest. I squirmed in my chair.

Harry noticed my comfort level had decreased, "You'd be squatting over him," he said, "so you'll be controlling the thrust and depth. Go as deep and slow as you want."

I knew the question of anal was going to come about at some point yet I still felt unsure about my feelings to it. In my private life it had never really been something which interested me. Sure I'd had people ask, before, but we'd never gone through with it. Usually I managed to put them off the idea by changing tact to get them to finish the job too soon. I little smile on my face as I promised it to them 'next time'. Most of the time, the thought of the act was enough to get them to the edge. With a little help from my mouth or hands they'd go spilling over said edge.

"If you're that against the idea, we don't have to go for it. I'm not one of those guys who likes to pressure women into doing things they're not comfortable with but - if you do - they'll be an extra five hundred in it for you…"

In my mind I was already running through various 'tests' I could do that afternoon, when I got home. Start small with, maybe, a finger and move up from there. If I liked it - I could try it for real on the shoot. If I didn't, I could turn the extra cash down.

"Can I think about it?" I asked.

"Sure. Take as long as you want. We can always start with the other scenes and save that for last." He turned to Tom, "You could always pull out and cum on her ass cheeks." Tom nodded, still smiling.

"The sex would need to be protected," I said.

"He has an up to date certificate," Harry said. Most in the industry carried certificates with them to prove they were clean but I still didn't like the idea of no condom. It was the one rule I promised myself never to break.

"I'm sorry," I went to say...

"That's fine," Harry continued, "condom it is. We just want you to say yes. Would you be happy for him to pull the condom off before ejaculating? Maybe shoot his load on your ass or your breasts?"

I nodded, "Okay."

Both Harry and Tom smiled.

AN UNLAWFUL KILLING

I'm not sure how long I had stopped talking, reminiscing about what had happened, before I came 'to'. Harry was just staring at me, occasionally wincing from what must have been a hell of a shooting pain from his groin. I had been staring straight ahead, absent-mindedly twirling the small butt-plug round and round in his ass. I let go of it and it dropped, discoloured from both blood and shit, to the floor. I stood up and looked him in the eyes.

"I'd forgotten about that," I'd told him.

"Kill me..." he whined once more. The broken record of a pathetic man begging to be put out of his misery like a limp animal. I think not.

"Did you forget?" I asked. He didn't answer. Not even sure whether he heard me. "About my friend?" I continued. Again - no facial expression from Harry suggesting he knew what I was talking about.

Talking about what had happened - how we had met - I can't believe I have only just remembered my friend. Another life lost because of these assholes. I'd left the so-called 'interview' in the coffee-shop feeling uneasy about the whole meeting. It was one thing to be promised a stack of money but - that didn't ensure I'd be safe from possible trouble. Richard's words played through my tired mind.

"And don't forget - you should take your own chaperone," he had advised. "If a company says 'no', that they don't want you to take someone with you, then walk away. A legit company wouldn't think twice about permitting it. Some, like me, would even advise it."

"Like hired security?" I had asked him.

"Could even be a friend," he'd replied, "just so long as someone is with you and knows you're safe."

My mind drifted to my friend, one of my oldest friends. His name was John.

Was John.

He was dead now. And it was because of these fucks.

Harry started to laugh through the pain. For the first time since being hit with the hammer, he looked directly at me. Eye to eye. A smile, that fucking smile, etched on his pained face. "How could I forget?" he laughed, "He screamed. He begged for his life. Even cried."

I turned away; scared that he could see the upset in my face, the tears in my eyes. Shake it out of your system. Forget it (for now at least). Make them suffer. Make John proud from wherever he lies. Make him proud. I turned back to Harry, "You've begged me tonight," I whispered. "Is that how my friend sounded? You've cried too...Another uncanny impression of my friend?"

John hadn't begged for anything. Harry was just trying to get a rise out of me. He nearly managed it too. Nearly. I know John didn't beg because they hadn't given him a chance to do so. They didn't give him the privilege. They snuck up on him and they killed him.

"Fuck you," Harry hissed. "Why don't you do the world a favour and kill yourself?" he spat. "Shit for blood, you're nothing but a waste of oxygen."

"Because of you," I reminded him.

"Kill yourself and be with your boyfriend."

"My boyfriend? John? No. You're mistaken. John was my friend."

* * * * *

John looked at me with wide eyes. I'm pretty sure he didn't know whether to believe me, or not. Not that I'd ever joked about things like this in the past. In fact, I don't think I'd ever spoken about my normal sex life in the past. Not since finding out he had a 'thing' for me anyway.

John was a friend who'd stuck with me since school. We went to college together and still remained friends when he went on to university and I went on to drama school. Once he had told me that he loved me. I guess he hoped I would have said I felt the same but I didn't. He was always just a good friend to me. Why would I want to ruin that with messy feelings of love? He was like a brother to me. A protective brother who I could discuss anything with. Which is one of the reasons I wanted to tell him about my move into the adult film industry.

"Your mum and dad don't know about it, I'm guessing?" he said, when he finally managed to string a sentence together.

I shook my head, "Only you."

"And this is what you want to do with your life?" he asked.

I had already worked on three 'assignments' and I felt comfortable with what I was doing. I actually felt as though I was at home on the sets, strange as it may sound. I'm sure there are others in the industry who don't feel this way - perhaps they even feel used by the system - but, so far, I was having a ball.

"So - what are the names of the films you've done?" he asked, a cheeky grin on his face.

"Don't!" I gave him a playful slap on the arm. I knew what was running through his mind; a sneaky viewing of my films. "If you ever come across them…"

He started to laugh. I rolled my eyes.

"Very good," I continued, "if you ever see the films - you can't watch them. Promise me."

"What? Deny myself the chance to sleep with you?" he laughed.

"You're disgusting!" I gave him another playful slap on the arm. I knew he was just teasing me.

"Look - if you're happy, and you're safe...I'm pleased for you. I'm surprised," he continued, "fucking surprised, to be honest, but - if it's what you want...Well...Good for you. Your secret is safe. Just promise me one thing," he finished.

"What?"

"Be safe."

I smiled at him and gave him a kiss on the cheek, "You're sweet."

"I mean it, if there is anything you ever need, give me a ring."

* * * * *

Harry spat, "You think it's my fault that your friend is dead? You're wrong."

"I beg your pardon?"

"It's your fault. You killed him. You invited him to the set. You told him to be there. You brought him along to his death. You're to blame." Harry laughed. "You killed your friend. Just as you killed everyone else. Just how much blood is on your hands?"

It was Harry who killed him. Harry and his friends. Not me. Yet - part of him - was right. A small part admittedly but there was some truth in his sentence. I had taken John along. I did take him to his death. Once again I shook the thoughts from my mind before putting my hands around Harry's neck. I applied pressure as hard as I could, cutting off his circulation. His skin went purple as his eyes bulged. I want to show him exactly what I felt but - in the meantime - there's no harm in showing him what John went through in his last moments.

* * * * *

I was sitting on the edge of the bed in the middle of what looked to be an abandoned warehouse. I was wearing the cat-suit as had been requested but this wasn't the reason I felt uncomfortable. The bed in the warehouse (heated with small heaters dotted around the room) was the reason I felt uncomfortable. It just felt unprofessional. Seedy. Even the cameras, three of them in total, set up around the room to capture various angles in one take, looked as though they were bottom end of the market. Had it not been for the fact they had given me the money as soon as I had walked in, with John on my arm, I'd have believed they couldn't afford me.

John was on a small plastic chair next to the wall. A few people milling around him with drinks in their hands, taking sips, as we waited for the action to begin. Looking around I didn't know any of the faces here (other than John, Tom and Harry) and couldn't tell what their roles were either.

Probably the busiest set I'd ever been on. I guessed three would be on camera, obviously Harry would direct and Tom would be my co-star but there were two extra people who just seemed out of place. Neither tried to talk to me or John which didn't help with making me comfortable. And speaking of comfort - John looked as though he was really out of place. He kept shifting in his chair as though desperate to get up and leave. Even the sight of me, my breasts spilling from the cat-suit, failed to get a reaction from him - something which surprised me considering the way he often spoke to me if I dared bare any flesh.

"Sorry," I mouthed to him.

He winked - almost as though to say everything was cool but I knew it wasn't.

Tom sat next to me. He was wearing jeans and a white tee shirt - no shoes or socks - and seemed perfectly at ease with where the shooting location was.

"Is it always in a warehouse?" I asked him, referring to the shoot.

"We move around a lot," he said.

"Any ideas when we're going to start?" I asked him.

"Soon. Just waiting to take care of something." He smiled. For some reason, hard to put my finger on it, his smile set me on edge as much as the film set had. From across the room John made a funny yelping sound which caught my attention. I turned to face him and screamed when I saw that a man was standing behind him clutching either end, of what looked to be wire, looped round John's neck. John's face was purpling by the second and his eyes were bulging from his skull as his arms flapped about pointlessly. I went to jump up - to run across to help him - but Tom grabbed me around the waist and pinned me to the bed.

"Watch your friend," he sneered in my ear, "watch the life slip away from him."

I was crying out for John, screaming how sorry I was, as we both continued to struggle against the people pinning us down. Panic shooting through my body as I realised no one was coming to help. Worse than that, some of the bystanders were watching the scene unfold with their dicks in their hands - stroking them in time with John's gasps.

Soon enough - as one man shot his load onto the concrete floor with a sigh of pleasure - the man strangling John let go of the wire and John's body slumped (lifeless) to the floor. I screamed before I felt a pair of hands wrap around my own neck; a fear that I was going to go the same way as John.

* * * * *

It took every ounce of willpower I had to stop from throttling Harry to death there and then. I released my hands from his neck as tears streamed down my face. He gasped for breath - a disappointed look on his face (I believe) that I hadn't just let him die. I wanted to. God only knows I wanted to but I couldn't. Not yet. Not like that. It was too easy for him. Too peaceful compared to what he (they) did to me. I owed it to myself - and the girls who'd been before me - to make him suffer.

"You don't get away with it that easily," I told Harry as I took a couple of steps away from him. "No way do you get away with it that easily. You're going to suffer like no other person has suffered before and - given what you do to people, what you did to people - that is saying something."

I reached down to the floor and picked the hammer up.

"I remember the first hit," I told him.

* * * * *

Tom let go of my throat and I gasped for air. He'd put so much pressure on, for so long, that my vision had started to blur and I started to see stars. I looked to the side, to see if anyone was going to help me but no one was coming. Instead - they were all cheering. Some of them (the on-lookers) were standing with their pants pooling round their ankles. Harry was busy flicking the cameras on.

"Careful, guys, you don't want to shoot your load too soon," he laughed as he ran to the next camera, "you've paid a lot to be here, may as well get your monies worth."

I turned back to Tom, still sitting on top of me, and went to beg for him to get off. His fist was clenched and held up high. Before I could get any words out, before I could utter a single sound, he brought the fist crashing down onto the side of my face. I screamed from both the pain and the shock; the first time I'd ever been punched in my life. I prayed for him to get off, I prayed for him to stop but he didn't. He raised his fist again and brought it back down.

* * * * *

Harry's scream filled the room as I hammered him directly on his left kneecap.

"I'm curious," I shouted over his cries, "how much did they pay to stand there and watch what you had planned for me? How much was I worth?" I didn't need Harry to confess the exact price. I knew it wasn't going to be a cheap rate - not with the money he'd offered me for coming along; although I knew as soon as the first blow connected with my face that I wasn't going to be getting paid. "How much was I worth?" I asked him again as I brought the hammer crashing down onto his other kneecap. Another satisfying scream filled the room, along with the horrendous sound of cracking bone. I wasn't sure how he organised such events and I knew I'd never get to know. I didn't care. It bothered me that I'd never find the men who'd paid to visit the set to - basically - jerk themselves off whilst watching Tom and I but I hoped they'd disappear back under the rocks they came from if Harry was no longer around to invite them to such trips. The most important thing for me, since starting this, was to ensure Harry and his gang paid the ultimate price.

I'd lost count of the number of blows I'd taken from Tom. I wonder if Harry will lose track of the amount of hits he suffers too or whether he'll remember each and every one up until the minute I take his life? I raised the hammer again and swirled it around in my hand so that the edge - the bit used to remove nails from walls - was pointing downwards. Without a second hesitation I brought it down into his shoulder. He screamed again. I hope he remembers the hits. I hope he remembers each and every last one of them.

* * * * *

I opened my eyes. Not sure how long I'd been out for. I tried to move but couldn't. My arms and legs stretched out; bound to the bed by cold, hard chains. I started to cry when I remembered where I was and what had happened.

I was still in the cat-suit. The front zipper was undone, exposing my breasts. And I must have been exposed around my crotch too, given the cool air breathing against it. I pulled at the restraints, desperate for them to break or come undone at least, but there was no movement in them.

I wailed out. A hope that someone would take pity on me.

Harry's voice came from the corner of the room – invisible from my position on the bed, "And ACTION!"

Panicked, I looked from side to side to see if I could see him. My heart skipped a beat when a handful of masked men walked into the room wearing nothing but red velvet robes. They approached the bed, without saying anything, and I realised the robes were open at the front with no clothes on underneath. Each man was either semi or completely erect. They stood around the bed, without blocking the view from the previously-positioned camera. It was then that I realised that the people I'd seen earlier - the ones I believed to be part of the crew - they were all nothing but spectators. They only 'filmmakers' had been Tom and Harry. Everyone else was just here for the 'entertainment' factor. More panic. Slowly, the ones at the foot of the bed moved to the side to make room for another masked man. Unlike the previous - this one was wearing a black velvet robe. Like the other men, there were no clothes underneath, just an erect penis and a pair of Dr Martin boots.

"Please. Let me go. I'm scared," I stuttered over my words. Could taste blood in my mouth.

The black robed man climbed onto the bed and moved up until his body was pressing against mine. With no words, and with the help of his left hand, he thrust hard into my arse - holding my leg up as far as the restraints permitted with his right hand in order to help with the angle. I screamed out in pain and continued to do so with each of his hard thrusts. The men standing around the bed stroking their cocks gently - as though not wanting to get too carried away until the black-robed man was near completion. My mind darted to the horrific possibility that, when this man was done, they'd each take it in turn too. I closed my eyes and continued to scream as he continued to pound.

Just as quickly as he started, he suddenly pulled out. I waited for him to roughly penetrate me again but the penetration didn't come. Was that it?

THE FILM

"That wasn't it though, was it? That was just the beginning. And what you've suffered so far, that's just the beginning too." I bent back down to my bag of toys and dropped the hammer in. Seconds later I pulled out some garden shears. I stood up to my full height and laughed as I gave them a test 'cut' by slicing through the air. Snip. Snip.

"Wh-what are you doing?" Harry stammered over his words. More music to my ears.

"What do you think?" I asked. I opened the shears up and moved them down to his cock so that a blade was on either side of it. I closed the shears up - just enough - to ensure the blades were touching skin.

"Ready?" I asked him.

"Please...Don't..."

I laughed. I had no intention of using the shears on his penis. It's not as though they cut my vagina with them...

* * * * *

"Open your eyes," I recognised Tom's voice. He was the man in the black-robe. I opened my eyes slowly. The men around the bed were still watching me, still with pricks in hand. Tom was standing, still masked, at the foot of the bed. He had a pair of scissors in his hand. "These men here have paid a lot of money to watch this," he explained, "and they want a show. Not much of a show if you keep your eyes closed."

"Please let me go."

"Ssh! They want to hear your moans. They want to hear your screams. They don't want to hear your pleas for mercy."

I fought again against the restraints - still with no joy.

Tom crawled up the bed, holding the scissors up, and ran the cold (open) blades against my bruised cheeks, across my neck, down my bosom. I shivered with fear and nervous anticipation all the way. Tom leaned down and suckled on my breast; my body betraying me with a sudden stiffening of the nipple. He sat up and smiled at the effect his mouth had had. He held the scissors up and opened them up to their fullest potential. A wink from his left eye. With no warning, no words, he moved the scissors down to my breast and clamped the blades shut on my nipple. I screamed as blood immediately dribbled from the fresh (sore) wound. The men around the bed - wanking their pricks furiously.

* * * * *

Harry screamed as loudly as I had when I cut his pink nipple off too - using the garden shears. I didn't stop at the one nipple, though, like Tom had done with me. I moved on to the second and - snip - sliced it from his shaking body. His first scream hadn't even had a chance to die down and so just continued into a longer, more drawn out one.

"Hurts, doesn't it?" I said.

Harry was still screaming. I still wasn't done. Tom had stopped at the one nipple before discarding the scissors and moving on but - no - that wasn't enough for Harry. I wanted him to feel what I felt but, more so, I wanted him to feel more. The pain for people who'd gone before me. I remembered what he'd said, on the film set, when he leaned in close to me whilst they set up another take - having terminated the recording temporarily.

* * * * *

"Who likes Period Play?" Tom was asking the group as they continued playing with themselves. Period Play was another strange fetish that some men had (and women, I guess). Men eating out of a woman on her period, before fucking her. The end shot being that of a bloody pussy; a sticky cream-pie of blood and semen.

Harry was undoing my restraints.

He leaned in close to me and smiled, "Keep up the good work," he whispered, "your fear smells lovely," he breathed in deeply.

* * * * *

"Can you smell your own fear? Does that smell as nice as my fear did?" I asked. "Does it turn you on? Make your horny for me?" I lifted the garden shears to his nose and opened them up; his nose soon between the blades. "I'm feeling generous," I told him as I held the shears against his skin. "If you want to breathe in through your nose one last time…"

He was screaming before I'd applied any pressure. The scream continued, echoing through the room, as his nose dropped to the floor in a bloody, pulpy mess.

I took a step back, looking at his face. Blood pouring from the fresh hole in his face, leaking into his gaping mouth as he continued to strain his vocal chords. He started to splutter on the blood as he spat mouthful after mouthful onto the floor.

"I thought you liked blood?" I asked. A fact I had learned from the set of the film.

* * * * *

"You're free!" Harry said as he walked away with the restraints.

I summoned all the strength I had and rolled from the bed. I landed, hard, on all fours on the concrete floor. Slowly - aching - I started crawling towards the warehouse's exit. Looking behind me, the men were all watching. Tom was the only one who was following, slowly, behind me.

Harry called out from next to the camera. His voice stole my attention and I saw him hit the recording button once more, "I vote yes for the Period Play, my good friend."

I turned to Tom, still crawling forward, and watched as he both smiled and nodded. He quickened his pace and - when close enough - lashed out with his booted foot. I shrieked, as it connected with my undercarriage, and I fell forward onto my stomach where I immediately rolled into a tight ball. Tom reached down and grabbed my legs by the ankles. He pulled my legs apart, exposing my vagina to both himself and the voyeurs near-by. I struggled to break free from his grip but couldn't - the pain turning all limbs to jelly. A sadistic grin on his face, he stamped down with his foot. Another scream. Tom looked down at smiled wider. Keeping my legs held apart, he took a side step to show the others what he could see.

"We have blood!"

A cheer from the men as Tom dropped to his knees and buried his face into my pussy.

* * * * *

Harry was unconscious. The shock of what I'd been doing obviously taking its toll on his body and state of mind. Still not enough yet. Still nowhere near enough. Now, though, is a good time to undo the restraints. We're gearing up towards the end and, for that, I need him on the floor. Ideally on all fours but I doubt he'll be cooperative. Regardless - need him off the pillar.

I walked out of the main room into the back area where I'd earlier slipped into the cat-suit. My clothes were hanging over the door. I pulled the jeans down and fished around in the pockets until I found what I was looking for - a small, silver key. The key to his freedom. His freedom from the restraints that is. There is no escaping this warehouse. He will die in here.

I took the key back into the main room and approached Harry's pillar. His head was still slumped down - clearly still unconscious. Good. It'll be easier to do this without the possibility of using his new-found freedom to lash out at me although I'm pretty sure I've stopped any chance of that happening with the previous blows to his shoulders and kneecaps, with the hammer. To be sure, I'll give his limbs another pounding with the hammer - ensure the job is done properly. Don't want him running away from me - like I had done from them when the opportunity presented itself.

I undid the top padlocks and unwound the chains. The top half of his body slumped forward - secured in place only by the ones around his legs. I crouched down and removed the lower padlocks too, before sliding the bottom chains off and dropping them to the floor with a satisfying 'clank'. He fell forward, face first, and landed in a broken heap on the floor. No surprise there. Had it been someone I cared for, I would have put something soft down for him to land on. Tough shit if it hurt.

I dropped the padlock onto the chains and walked to the front of the pillar, next to where he was slumped. I picked the hammer up, which wasn't too far from where he lay, and cracked it down (hard) on his kneecaps again. One at a time. I didn't stop at his kneecaps, though. It was still entirely possible for him to lash out at me with fists. After all, I hadn't touched his hands yet.

I re-positioned myself on the floor next to his hands. With my left hand I reached down and turned his hands around so they were palm down on the floor. A hard enough hit and I believe I can break all of his fingers and knuckles in a single blow. I put pressure on his wrist to stop his hand from moving and raised the hammer high in the air, with my other hand. I closed my eyes and brought it down hard. A crack. Funny time to get squeamish but there was something about the sound of breaking bones which repulses me. Even when it was bones belonging to someone who deserved them to be broken, like Harry. Can't be squeamish now, though. Just need to keep going until there is no risk of him trying to punch me. I raised the hammer again and continued to hit the hands individually until they no longer resembled hands.

A few hits more.

I dropped the hammer, satisfied that I'd done enough.

"Now wake up, you fuck."

* * * * *

"Cut the cameras," Tom called across to Harry who duly did as Tom had instructed. Funny. I thought Harry was the director.

"What is it?" Harry called out.

Tom removed his mask and dropped it at my side.

"Fucking bitch is out cold."

"What?!" I heard Harry walk over. I didn't open my eyes. Just laid still. Carried on pretending to be out for the count, wouldn't have had to pretend if I hadn't taken action. Every time I had tried to push him away, from where he lapped between my bloodied legs, he'd reached up and slammed my head back against the concrete; enough to daze me, enough to stop me from fighting back, enough to stop me from ruining their shot.

"Was just trying to stop her from fighting back," Tom said.

"She fucking dead?"

I felt Tom's fingers on my neck.

"Because," Harry continued, "if she's dead, that's a lot of money right there, you know what I'm saying?" he hissed. His voice was low. No doubt wanting to keep the possibility of my death a secret from the perverts watching from a few feet away.

"What's going on?" one of the men shouted.

"Is she fucking dead?" Harry hissed.

"No," he said, "there's a pulse."

"You're fucking lucky. Because that would have come out of your cut."

"What's going on?" the voice from the back piped up again.

I heard Harry step away from me. More footsteps behind him as Tom followed. Harry's voice was muffled as he explained something to the group of spectators. I strained harder to listen to what was being said.

"Who's Mr. Stone?"

"I am."

"You got the cash?"

"Over there."

"All there or do I have to count it?"

"Always insult your guests?"

Harry apologised. "Tom, get the bag."

I heard Tom's footsteps get fainter as he walked to the other side of the warehouse to - I presume - where the money was. Payment for coming along and watching? I wanted to turn my head to see what was going on but I couldn't. I couldn't risk them seeing I was awake. I couldn't risk the punishment starting again.

"We're good," Tom called out.

"Okay so - as agreed - when the time comes you're the one who gets to pull the trigger...And I'll throw in a bonus, if you want to go on camera - you can fuck her any which way you want too."

"Really?"

"Sure - think of it as an apology for the remark about counting the money."

"Any way I want?"

"Friend - if you want - you can do it after she's dead. As long as it goes on camera, I don't give a fuck."

My heart skipped a beat. I turned my head to the side and opened my eyes. They were all grouped together. The majority of them had their backs to me. If I don't make a move for it - I'm as good as dead. I need to make a run. I need to escape. Summoning all of my strength, I rolled onto my front and pushed myself to all fours before standing. The pain was unbearable; not a single part of me that didn't ache.

"She's awake!" Tom called out.

I looked at him, he was in the corner of the room next to a bag (I presume of money). Don't waste time, don't hang about, just go. I started to run towards a door closest to me - thankfully one which had the sign 'exit' illuminated above it.

"Stop her!" Harry shouted.

More footsteps running behind me. I didn't waste time in looking. Just kept running. My body slammed against the door - the large push handle - and I spilled out into the road. I was in a large industrial estate; one road in and one road out. I knew I didn't have the strength in me to run far enough to ensure I was safely away from them. Especially considering they were right behind me. Only one option; the river across the road and behind the barrier. I ran as fast as I could, scared of stumbling and scared of them catching up with me. Without thinking, knowing how close they were, I vaulted over the barrier and down into the cold, cold waters.

ESCAPED

The water was freezing and took my breath away. I broke the surface and took a deep breath. I needed to disappear. Full of as much air as I could take in, I submerged myself under the water's surface once more - in time to see faces leaning over the barrier.

Can't go back up. Can't go back up. Can't let them see me. Hopefully it's dark enough to make me near invisible. Hopefully the water is murky enough to hide me...I started to swim, keeping as close to the wall as the weeds on the river bed permitted. I wasn't sure what was keeping me moving, I didn't know why this strong survival instinct had kicked in. My mind seemed clear - other than the single thought 'survive'. No thoughts about my mother and father, no thoughts about my childhood, no other memories (or regrets) flashing through my tired mind. Just survive.

Starting to run out of air. How easy would it be to just stop. Stop struggling, stop trying not to breathe in the filthy water, just drown. Certainly more peaceful than the death waiting for me at the warehouse. I deserve a bit of peace. I deserve some quiet.

Mum and dad flashed through my mind, smiling, happy, a time of us playing together from my childhood, sitting on beach towels on the sandy beach. I recalled that it was Tenerife when I was nine, or ten, years old. Thoughts of them weeping at my funeral. No coffin. Body never found. I simply disappeared. Can't do that to them. Can't.

I broke the surface of the water and took a huge gasp of air. I half expected to hear them call out my location but I didn't hear anything. I looked around. Had gone further than I'd thought I had. I can't see them. I can't hear them either. I wanted to get out of the water but didn't dare. Can only keep swimming along the water's edge. Far enough to know I'm safe. Far enough to take me closer to civilisation.

I kept edging my way as far as I could go, shivering the whole way. I knew my best bet was to swim across to the other side of the river and climb out there. Over there, I'd be safe. I couldn't bring myself to do it though. I couldn't. My limbs were aching and the freezing waters were numbing my joints. Every other week this year there'd been various stories, in the papers, about youths drowning in the river. They'd get drunk, according to the reports, and dare each other to swim across just to disappear under the water's ripples at the half way point. Their bodies found the following day by police divers. Water in their lungs. If I tried to swim across, now. I wouldn't make it.

Another memory of a happier time spent with my family flashed through my mind; laughing in the back garden on a hot summer's evening. Dad was cremating some burgers on the disposable barbecue mum had bought with the monthly shop - just as she did whenever there was good weather. She'd wanted a real barbecue - a nice one - but dad put his foot down. He said there was no point due to the fact that the weather in this country was so unpredictable. By the time we'd come to use it, the next time we had good weather, it would be rusted and broken. Much easier to just get the cheap disposables.

The wall I had been edging along stopped. Instead it was more weeds leading the way to a bank I could easily climb up. I didn't make a move for it, though. Not immediately. I stayed flat against the wall - my eyes scanning the river bank for any signs of movement, any signs of people waiting for me to suddenly appear from the water. I'm not sure how long I waited - watching the side - but it felt like forever. My body was stinging now - not just from the blows I had sustained but because of the water too. There were no signs of movement. Slowly I pulled myself from the water. Thankful to get onto dry land - the latex cat-suit had been made much heavier by the water.

On the bank, I wanted to crash on the mud and sleep until morning - maybe longer - but I couldn't. Just because they're not here now, looking for me, it doesn't mean they won't be on their way. No doubt throwing some clothes on so as not to attract unwanted attention if there is anyone else out here at this time of night. I stumbled across the mud, my feet sinking in as I did so. A few more feet and I was on the pathway which lead to the road.

I started to run.

Can't slow down now.

As I continued to run towards what I hoped to be civilisation, I couldn't help but keep checking behind me. I was expecting to see people chasing behind or a car on the horizon speeding towards me and yet - each time I turned - there was nothing. Just blackness and emptiness. Regardless of the lack of people following, it didn't stop me from continuing to run as hard and fast as I could despite the feeling that my lungs were about to burst from within my beaten chest.

I jumped at the sound of someone shouting from nearby. Breathing so heavily, as I continued to fight off the exhaustion, I had missed what they initially said. They called out again and I span round in the direction of the voice.

"I said are you okay?" they called out again.

"Please help me," I said.

It was an older looking woman. She was sitting in a car, parked up by the side of the road on the opposite side to where I was. She climbed out of the car. My first thought was that she was one of them - I don't know, a wife, perhaps? Waiting patiently for them to finish doing what they'd obviously paid to take part in so she could give them a lift back home again? No. A silly idea. No one would support their partner to do that.

"What's happened?" she asked as she hurried over to me. As she neared I dropped to my knees. So tired. I can't go on. If she is one of them - or anything to do with them - it doesn't matter. There's nothing I can do about it. I have no more fight left in me. I'm done. If there is where it ends then so be it. I started to cry. As she neared I felt her hand on my shoulder - no pressure - just a gesture to let me know she was there. I looked up, teary-eyed, and saw the horrified look on her face when she saw the state I was in. I probably look like Hell. My face aching from the hits I had sustained, my jaw throbbing, I can still taste blood in my mouth despite thinking I'd washed most of it away when I landed in the water. The look on her face was important though - it told me that she was definitely not one of them. It told me that she had compassion. She had empathy. And - more importantly - she was shocked.

"Please help me..." I stammered through my tears.

"My poor girl what happened?" she helped me to my feet. "Come on, it's okay..." She helped me towards the car. We walked around it and she helped me into the passenger seat. I yelped in pain as she sat me down - and again when she put the seat belt around me. She slammed the car door and ran round to the driver's side. She hopped in and closed the door before firing up the engine. "It's okay," she reassured me, "I'll get you to the hospital..."

"No!"

"What?"

"No hospital. Please."

"You need..."

"Please..."

The woman looked at me. A genuine - welcome - look of concern on her face. She nodded, "Okay...then...where do you want me to take you?" she asked.

* * * * *

"She took me home and waited with me as I had asked. My good samaritan. I ran in, threw some clothes on and came back down with a handful of clothes thrown into a bag. Took me home. I mean - to my mum and dad's home. She kept saying she thought I needed to go to the hospital but I was worried you'd come looking for me there - and at my own home. Neither place felt safe. Only mum and dad's home...Only that felt safe to me." I looked at Harry. He was still out for the count. Hadn't heard a damned word I was saying. Didn't matter though. He wouldn't have cared about these details. The fact he sold the lives of innocent people to the rich and perverted - that showed he didn't care about the little details. To him, we weren't people. We weren't human. We were just play-things. "That woman," I continued regardless, "...What you did to me...In that brief time with you and your friends...made me forget that people like that existed. Good people. Caring."

Harry started to groan as he laid there on the floor. Slowly he was coming round. As he became more conscious of his surroundings his groans became louder and more pained. I smiled.

PORN

* * * * *

I woke up in pain. Just as I had fallen asleep in pain, with mum sat on the edge of the bed stroking my ankle (for comfort I believe). They had been shocked - both mum and dad - when I had knocked on the door late the previous night after my good samaritan dropped me off. They offered her money - as a thank you for bringing me to them - but she refused it. She just reiterated the fact that she believed I should have gone to hospital before she wished me well. Both mum and dad agreed with her - something they told me after they'd thanked the woman and seen her on her way.

"She's right," dad said, "we should take you to the hospital..."

"What happened?" mum asked.

I didn't say anything. Growing up we had the rule; if someone wanted to talk about something they would bring it up. They wouldn't need to be asked. Asking was prying.

We were sitting in the living room. Or rather, I was sitting. Mum and dad were standing by the door. Dad was putting his coat on, ready to take me to the hospital. I realised that this was one of those occasions where the rule was disregarded.

"I'm fine," I said, "I just want to go to bed and sleep it off."

Mum and dad didn't move.

"What happened?" mum asked again.

"I don't want to talk about it," I told her. I told them both.

"I think we need..."

"Please. I just want to go to bed."

I tentatively got up from the chair and made my way past them and up the stairs. They followed to the bottom of the stairs and watched as I disappeared around the landing and towards my old childhood bedroom. I was thankful when they didn't follow. In the bedroom, I closed the door behind me and made my way across to the bed. I laid down - carefully - and wept into the pillow.

That night was spent tossing and turning. Thoughts going round and round in my head of what I'd been through that night and what I should do about it. Even how it came to be in the first place? So many film sets - how'd I end up on that one? In the early hours I found myself hunched over the toilet throwing up into the bowl as the thoughts continued to play havoc with both my mind and my body.

"Everything okay in there?" mum knocked on the door.

"I'm fine..."

"Need a glass of water?"

I was already drinking from the tap, cleansing the harsh taste from my mouth. I contemplated going to the police and reporting the crime but I knew it would just be inviting more trouble. Besides, Harry and his friends...They'd have cleaned the scene up now. They'd have removed all trace on the off-chance that I did go to the authorities. They looked professional, with what they were doing. They wouldn't leave any traces of what they did. They weren't that stupid. Besides, the police would need to know all the details, there'd be a possibility of mum and dad discovering the films I'd been a part of. On top of everything else - I can't risk them finding out. I can't risk them turning their backs on me. I'll get over this. Somehow. I'll move on. Not sure how but I will. Mum and dad disowning me? I couldn't get over that. The fact that they were in my head when I thought I was a dead girl...That showed how much I cared for them. Not that I ever doubted it. I can't imagine a life without them.

* * * * *

Harry was fully conscious and in excruciating agony - just as I had planned. I moved over to where he was lying on the floor and laid myself down next to him.

"If you die..." I corrected myself, "...When you die...Do you think anyone will miss you?" I asked him. He didn't answer me, just carried on groaning in pain. I think the days of him answering me back, conversing with me, are over. A shame. I liked him begging. I carried on, "I miss my friend. The one you killed. My mum. My dad. They would have missed me." I paused, "I'm sure the other girls - the one your friend told me about - I'm sure they will be missed too even though their friends and families don't know what has happened to them. People will still care. People will still hope they're okay." Another pause. "Friends? Friends. Do you miss your friend?" I whispered to him.

He groaned. I'll take that as a 'yes'.

ONE DOWN

I was going through my agent's emails on his computer system. He hadn't been in when I knocked on the door to his small office within a complex. I had tried the handle and had been surprised to find it unlocked. It either meant he'd popped out, maybe to collect his mail from the reception, or he was forgetful and hadn't locked it the previous night. Hopefully the latter. All I knew from that evening was the first names of the scum who had hurt me. No surnames. It made searching through his many emails a time consuming process.

Of course I had started with a search on my name. I thought it would be easier to find the initial email Frank had sent me (offering me the job) but I couldn't even find that. Plenty of emails to and from me but - not that one.

"Come on...Where is it?" I sat back in Frank's comfortable leather chair and threw my hands in the air. Nothing. Can't find anything. "Shit!"

"What the fuck are you doing here?"

I jumped at the sound of Frank's voice. I looked up and saw him standing there, in the doorway to his own office. His arms folded. He looked angry.

"Get the fuck out of here," he hissed at me.

"Where is it?" I asked him. My tone hinted that I wasn't messing around. Just as his tone suggested the same to me. I didn't care about his tone. I just wanted the details of the people who had hurt me and - if anything - he should have been thanking me that I had let him walk out of his apartment. I could have just killed him. As I was planning to do to his associates .

"I'm phoning the police." He stormed over to the desk and picked up his telephone.

I couldn't help but laugh.

"Fine. Phone them. Sure they'll be interested to know what you did to me," I laughed. "You and your friends. Tell me - how much money have you earned from me?"

He looked at me. Was that confusion on his face?

"And will you tell them what you did to me?" he slammed the phone down. "I should fucking kill you, you know? You're a whore. Nothing more and nothing less."

"Didn't you already try that?" I hissed back at him. Again - he just looked at me as though I had lost my mind. I had lost my mind?! He sold me out. He tried to have me killed and yet here he was thinking I was the one who was in the wrong.

"Not spoken to you since last night anyway, since the last shoot. How'd that work out for you?"

Was he being funny? Was he trying to build bridges? Was it a threat? If I don't leave him alone he'll arrange something else, similar, to happen to me?

"Is that supposed to be funny. Fuck you!"

Clearly I had run out of time on his computer - and in his office - I stood up and made my way towards the door. Frank reached out and grabbed me by the arm, stopping me in my tracks.

"Get the fuck off me!" I yelled.

"Ssh," he whispered. "I just want to know...Last night...You know I made an appointment with the doctor, right? You know - a health check...Were you joking?"

Oh. I got it. The sudden change in his tact was because he was concerned with what I had told him the previous night - the night I hopefully infected him. I smiled at him.

"You might want to cancel the doctor's appointment," I said.

His eyes lit up and he straightened his back. I do believe he is experiencing relief.

"Thank fuck for that. You know, you had me worried. Come on, sit, we can talk things through..."

What was his game? I felt confused.

"You didn't let me finish," I said. "I was saying, you might want to cancel the appointment and reschedule it for a couple of months down the line. The virus...It has an incubation period...Testing now will most likely yield a negative result..."

I smiled and pulled my arm from his grip. He had a shocked expression on his face as I stormed from the room and slammed the door shut. I hope - when the time comes - the result is positive.

I hope I've fucked his life just as he and his friends have fucked mine.

* * * * *

"Even if we had sat down and talked like he suggested," I said to the ever-groaning Harry, "and I had found out that he hadn't had a part to play in what had happened. It would have been too late to do anything about it. Couldn't wind the clock back to the previous night. Couldn't have un-fucked him..." I looked towards Harry as he continued to writhe around in agony. He wasn't looking very good. Not sure how much longer he has before he dies from shock. Long enough for me to finish. That's all that matters. I asked him, "If you could turn the clock back - would you change anything?" I asked him. "Would you undo what you did to me? Would you stop there? Would you go back and undo what you did to the other women too? Or are you happy with how life has turned out for you?" I laughed. "I don't think you are, are you? Probably give anything to turn that proverbial clock back a few months, maybe years - however long you've been doing this for."

I waited for him to say something - anything - but nothing came from his mouth but more groans and whining. When suffering, most animals would have been put to sleep hours ago. This is one animal who'll get to suffer every last minute until the last bit of breath escapes his lungs.

I stood up and walked over to the cameras - the sudden realisation that I hadn't checked on them for a while. Needed to make sure they still have battery power and sufficient recording space left. Don't want them to run out of recording potential before I've finished the film.

Red light still flashing.

H.D.D still half empty.

We're good.

"I wasn't sure what I was going to do when I left that office. Didn't know how I'd be able to track you down. In the end - you know what it was that lead me to all of you - nothing but luck. It was as though God wanted you punished just as much as I wanted you dead. You know what a nice feeling that is? To know that God wanted you hurt as much as I did? Knowing that made everything I did to your friend so much easier. Because it was justified."

* * * * *

I was parked up in the industrial estate. My heart was racing. I hadn't been here since that night. It was a while ago and yet everything seemed fresh in my mind. Just looking at the building - the one where it had all happened - brought everything back. The pain I had felt, the humiliation, watching my friend die and - of course - the fear of dying. I had thought that night was to be my last.

I opened the car door and threw up onto the pavement.

I don't even know why I am here. They won't be here. They're not that stupid surely, to come back to the scene of the crime. I doubt they'll ever come by this area again. Looking around, in the day light, I'm not even sure what this area is used for anymore. The area doesn't look like it's used for much now - no 'workers' around. No genuine workers at least. There's a couple of working girls standing next to containers; casually leaning around whilst waiting for business. Surprised they get any customers down here.

I was forced to eat my words when I saw a car pull up to one of the women. The woman sauntered over, the bottom of her arse cheeks showing from under the oh-so short mini-skirt. She leaned into the car and - just as quickly - she turned and walked away.

"Must be someone looking for directions," I muttered to myself.

The driver jumped out and hurried after her. My heart skipped at beat when I realised who it was. Tom. The actor. He grabbed the woman by her arm and turned her towards him. She slapped him hard across the face. He didn't retaliate. They were talking. I couldn't hear what was being said but wished I could.

What was he doing? Was he just horny? Looking for a fuck? Or was he fishing for more business for Harry and his paying customers? I couldn't take my eyes off them. He leaned in and hugged the woman. A second later and she was hugging him back. He fished in his pocket and pulled out what looked like a wad of notes. Holding it up, I watched in horror as the woman took the cash from him. His smile spread across his face. That fucking smile.

He walked her to the car and held the door open for her. She looked around, as though worried someone else would be watching or coming, and climbed in. Tom slammed the car door and ran around to his own side. He climbed in and the car sped off.

I quickly closed my own car door and started the engine before following (from a sensible distance). I half expected the car to turn down one of the many alleys so they could carry out their business transaction but was delighted when it didn't. It continued out of the industrial estate and onto the main road. Still I followed. Another car went on by - in the opposite direction - and flashed its lights. Tom sounded the horn. Not an angry held-down beep of his car's horn but more of a friendlier 'toot-toot'. In the rear-view mirror I saw the car turn into the industrial estate. Who was that? A friend on his way for a cheap encounter with a down and out? Just a coincidence? Another dirty rapist?

It wasn't just those questions bouncing around in my head. My mind was brimming with a whole load of 'what ifs'; what if he leads me to Harry, what if they're headed for another so-called film shoot, what if they do end up parked up in some seedy little car park, what if he spots me following and leads me to a trap...I ignored all of them. If I wanted any chance of revenge, if I wanted any sort of justice, I knew I'd have to keep following until they arrived at their destination. If not then I knew there'd most likely be another chance.

And so what if it is a 'film set', my brain answered my what-if question. I could phone the police, alert them as to what was going on. They'd show up and arrest all involved, hopefully in time to protect the girl.

We drove for thirty minutes - give or take - before we finally reached the destination. A cul-de-sac filled with modest looking houses. Tom drove straight in, with no hesitation, whereas I drove on by. Could hardly follow him right into his driveway. I turned into the next cul-de-sac and parked up. I nervously walked back to Tom's cul-de-sac. It didn't take long for me to see which house belonged to him; his car parked in the drive-way. It was weird - the houses around here looked normal. Not what I was expecting given the experiences I had shared with Tom. For some reason I pictured him having a large house in the middle of nowhere - maybe its own dungeon in the basement. This makes perfect sense, I guess. If he did have his own house - a house in the country - then I guess he'd have used that as the filming location. Less chance of being seen by - thinking back to the industrial estate - hookers touting for business.

PORN

* * * * *

"I'm not sure how long I waited outside his house for - hidden out of sight down one of the alleyways leading to a connecting cul-de-sac. I wasn't sure if I was going to be there all night or whether I was going to be there for five minutes. More to the point, I wasn't sure if I was just standing there - waiting - whilst a girl was getting tortured behind the closed door. You know how that made me feel?" I asked Harry. No answer. Just more moaning. "Imagine my relief when the front door finally opened and he came out - girl in tow. He loaded her back into the car - and they drove out of the cul-de-sac. You know, the two of them were actually smiling. Like they had had a nice time. Both had a nice time...That was a surprise to me. Half expected her to either not come out or come out covered in cuts and bruises - just as I had been left."

Harry coughed. Another moan. I'm pretty sure he is on the way out. Better move the story along for him. Don't want him missing the end of it. Don't want him missing the grand finale. I smiled as I considered what he had coming his way. I hope he can see it. I hope he can see what's coming - when I make the big reveal...I felt a tingle of excitement and tried to shake it off. Don't think about that now. Now isn't the time. Move the story on. Let him hear what happened to his friend.

* * * * *

The back door was open. Even if it hadn't been I wouldn't have let it deter me from getting in. I would have smashed the window and reached in to undo the lock. I wouldn't have cared if he'd seen it or whether the police had been called. It wouldn't have been important. All I could think about was hurting him. Hurting him and getting to Harry. I hurried through the kitchen - grabbing a couple of knives from the knife block on the side - and made my way up the stairs towards his bedroom.

Again, nothing strange in here. Nothing to hint at the type of person he really was. Nothing to even suggest that he was in the adult industry (was he even in the adult industry?) - everything just seemed normal. A large bed in the centre of the room; unmade from his encounter with the hooker. Two large wardrobes; both closed. Bedside cabinets either side of the bed - a picture on one of them. I walked over to it and picked it up. It was a photograph, professionally taken in a studio, of Tom cuddling a pretty blonde. They were both smiling. He was standing behind her with his arms around her - his hands interlocked. A wedding band. What? He's fucking married? After what he had done to me? After bringing that woman back to his home? Maybe he's separated. Yes. That must be it. They're no longer together. He still loves her - evident from the remaining photo - and has turned to hurting women as a way of dealing with the pain? Makes sense. That doesn't make any sense though...

There, on the other bedside cabinet, was make-up and a book. Some slushy romance, going by the title, clearly aimed at the female market. I moved across the floor to the cupboards and opened them up; one side contained men's clothes and the second half seemed to be women's. Maybe she's just moved out? Not yet taken the clothes. Or maybe she saw him for the monster he really is and - as a result - she's rotting away somewhere near by? I sniffed the air - nothing that smelt funky.

So is he a 'normal' family man? The monster who had hurt me, who had raped me...? He's your average Joe? The thought of him living a life and pretending to be 'normal' whilst hiding his dark secret scared me more than the idea of him being a sick business man living the life in every way possible. I don't know why. Maybe it was because it led to the possibility of more people being like him? If this 'normal' person is hiding this secret - what secrets do other seemingly normal people hide from the rest of us?

For the second time this evening I felt sick. Hold it in. Need to hide when he gets here. Need to take him by surprise. Can hardly do that if I line his floor with vomit.

* * * * *

I walked over to the pillar, where Harry had been previously bound, and scanned the area on the floor. There it is. The small butt-plug I'd earlier used to loosen Harry's rectum. I picked it up trying not to get a hold of the shit covered end.

"Nearly at the point where we're going to need to...Well...No sense ruining the surprise for you." I looked at him to see if there was any reaction. Nothing. His eyes were closed as he continued to roll from side to side - still in agony. I wonder if he even heard me? Not a problem if he didn't. He'll soon understand what's happening. Not long to go now.

With the plug in one hand, I took a hold of the bag of goodies with my spare hand and took them over to where Harry was sprawled out. I let go of the bag and positioned myself next to Harry's dirty rectum once more.

"I know what's coming," I told him despite knowing he wasn't really hearing me, "so I'll be nice again to show that despite what you did to me, there is still a part of me deep down admittedly, which does have feelings and care for the well-being of people."

"Please..." I could barely hear Harry's words as they came from his mouth, "kill me..."

I laughed. "I will. That you can count on. But not yet. Are you not even curious to know what I did to your colleague? Your so-called business partner? Not even a little bit?"

I reached down with the small plug and re-inserted it into Harry's arse. He barely registered it. So much pain going on in his body - it wouldn't surprise me if he couldn't. He'll be thankful though. Might not know it yet but he will definitely be thankful in the long run. Thankful for the stretching of his tender ring.

"Is that nice?" I asked him as I started gently fucking him with the toy. "Can you even feel it?" He didn't answer my question. I was a little disappointed at the lack of appreciation. Maybe I shouldn't have bothered with this little act of kindness. Perhaps I should have just continued with the story at hand.

PORN

* * * * *

I was hiding under the bed. My heart was beating so hard I thought he'd hear it the moment he walked into the bedroom. I was even paranoid that my breathing was too loud. I held my breath as he flicked the light switch on. He walked over to the bedside cabinet and turned the small lamp on. With that on, he returned to the doorway and killed the main light. The room was only illuminated by the small lamp now. The mattress groaned as he threw himself into the middle of the bed. A slight panic as it sagged towards me - a little part of me worried that I'd get crushed.

Despite putting myself into this position - I was scared. Scared of being discovered, hiding here, scared of making a mess of what I wanted to do, scared - I guess - that I wouldn't have the guts to go through with it. That I'd panic at the last minute and try and get away - something, I'm sure, I wouldn't manage. Not a second time. Especially now I know where he lives. If I don't go through with this...and if he discovers me - he'll make sure I don't live to try it another day. I need to go through with this. I need to make him suffer for what he had done to me.

I heard him move around on top of the bed before the light went out. More movement from the top of the bed as he made himself comfortable. I gripped the two knives in either hand and prepared myself...This is it. Now or never.

* * * * *

Still fucking Harry's arse, I hooked a knife from the bag and placed it against the skin of Harry's neck. He closed his eyes as he braced himself for the blade to slice his neck.

"Not yet," I told him as, with my other hand, I pulled the plug from his arse and threw it away. "I was hiding under Tom's bed waiting for him to turn the lights out. As soon as he did so, I moved out from where I was lurking...I placed the blade of one of the kitchen knives against his throat before flicking the bedside lamp on. Should have seen his face. His expression. When he saw me. He recognised me immediately. I won't lie, that made me happy...Saved me having to remind him of what he had done to me. Saved wasting time after all - I wasn't sure if his wife was due home...I wasn't sure if we were going to get interrupted. I just wanted to do what needed to be done and get out. In and out as quiet as possible. Not that I needed to be quiet. He screamed. Man did he scream."

CONFESSIONS

"What are you doing here?" Tom asked. Panic in his voice. Clearly a rhetorical question. He knew what I was doing there. He knew what was coming.

"Wanted to talk to you," I told him.

"Talk?"

"You seem surprised."

"What the fuck do you want to talk about?"

What was this? False bravado? He doesn't fool me. I can see the fear in his eyes. I can see he is uncomfortable with the situation and I can see in his eyes that he knows he isn't the one in control. In this instance - unlike the last time - the power was mine.

"I want to talk about that night," I told him, "I want to talk about what you did to me."

"It was just business," he said. He didn't sound as 'angry' now. In fact, he sounded as scared as he looked.

"Tell me more about the business," I ordered him. I wanted to know whether I was a one-off or whether it was a regular thing. I already knew the answer though. I already knew. The real question was - how many people had he seen before me? How many girls - whether they be prostitutes or actresses...How many girls hadn't made it off the film set? At least - made it out whilst they were breathing?

"It's just business."

"We've covered that. Tell me what happens. How does it work?"

"What?"

"I want to know. We never got to the end...I got scared and left if you remember. Have to be honest, thought you guys would have spent more time looking for me..."

"We did look for you. We thought you drowned."

"You didn't think of looking a little further down the river? That was a mistake you won't live to regret."

"What are you going to do?"

"You look scared."

"Fuck you."

"Are you scared?"

"Fuck you."

"I can see it in your eyes. It's not nice, is it? The knowledge that you're going to die. Not a nice feeling to have. Tell me - is your family flashing through your mind? Happier days you've previously lived? I didn't have that feeling immediately but - when I was in the river - I did have flashes…Made me want to live. Made me realise I had much to lose. Do you have much to lose? A pretty wife?"

"Fuck you."

Clearly not going to get much more from him continuing down this path. I changed tact, "Do you want to live? And, please, don't say fuck you again. Let's have an honest answer for a change - a straight answer. Do you want to live?"

"Yes."

"Then tell me about the business you run."

"People pay good money…"

"To what?"

"To watch. They like watching."

"Watching what? I want you to say it."

"To watch us hurt women."

"Why film it?"

"You think it's just the people who were there who wanted to see? We can only have a select few people on the site or else…Wrong people could get invited and…"

"You're scared of the police making an appearance. So what? You film it and offer people the chance to see it online? For a subscription of course?"

"Yes. Please. Move the knife."

"I don't think so." I pushed the knife against his throat harder. Must have cut the skin a little as a small trickle of blood ran down his throat and onto the pillow. Nothing a plaster won't fix. He winced in pain. I didn't take the pressure off.

"How much? The people who were there? How much did they pay?"

"A thousand."

"A thousand?" I felt sick. The thought that there were people out there who were willing to pay that sort of money just to watch someone get hurt (and killed). It's a sick world.

"And where do these people come from? How do you get that audience?"

"I don't deal with that side of things. I'm just the guy on camera...That's Harry's domain...Please...I've told you everything."

"No you haven't. There's still much to talk about."

"I heard Harry talking to someone. Apparently someone paid more to finish me off..."

"The golden ticket."

"The golden ticket?"

"He was the one who'd kill you, when the time came. He'd paid the most - in a bidding war via text…It was always the same; highest bidder got to pull the trigger."

I took a moment to try and make sense of it; to try and figure out why there were people out there who wanted to hurt others so badly that they'd pay good money to do so. It scared me that I couldn't think of an answer. Certainly not a sane one.

Keeping the knife against his throat, with the pressure applied, I crawled over him and laid down next to him. Pushing against him, I managed to move him onto his side so that I was behind him, still reaching around to keep the knife against him. He was shaking. Quite funny really - how pathetic he looked when the shoe was on the other foot. I wished I'd had a camera to record it. Something to remember him by in years to come when he was nothing but dust and bone.

"How much was my life worth?" I asked him. I wasn't sure that I wanted to know.

"Ten grand."

"Ten?" I wasn't sure what the value should have been but it seemed a lot for something which would have been over within a second - for the man pulling the trigger at least.

"How can I track these people down?"

"We don't have their details. Just numbers and they're deleted after each session. No connection. We use pay as you go phones and swap them after each film..."

"What? Then how do you build your audience?"

"The website. It's always through the site. When we want to make a new film, when we're ready, we advertise a new number...I swear..."

"What about your friend Harry?"

"I have his number. My business phone - the one downstairs on charge in the living room - it has his number stored. Please...Take it..."

"Oh I will."

I was disappointed that I wouldn't be able to track down all the people - at least, all the people who were on the set. I'd wanted to make them all pay but...Well...I wouldn't know where to start. The only reason I got here - to Tom - was sheer fluke.

"Want to know a secret?" I asked him. He didn't answer. Must have thought it a rhetorical question. "Before you got silly - you know, heavy footed - I enjoyed some of what you did to me...Actually enjoyed it. One bit in particular...You know which bit?"

"What?" he stuttered.

I purred in his ear, "I liked it when you fucked my ass."

He didn't say anything. His lack of response surprised me.

"You like it in the ass?" I asked him, breathing seductively into his ear. "It's okay - don't be shy...We're all friends, aren't we?" I repeated the question, "You like it in the ass more than the pussy?"

"Yes," he stuttered again.

"You want it in the ass now?" I asked him. "The girl, earlier - the one you picked up from the estate...Did she get it in the ass?"

"Yes."

"Did she enjoy it?"

"Yes."

"Make her cum?"

"I think so."

"You think so? You know - there's a g-spot in the man's ass...The prostate and if handled correctly...It can give the man a really powerful orgasm. Did you know that? I've been on some sets where the director wanted the man to experience it...And - I have to say - at first I was dubious...But having seen it with my own eyes...It's true. Some of the actors I worked with - they said it was the most intense orgasm they've ever had..."

"What are you doing?" he asked. What I was doing was running a plastic handled knife up and down his crack with my other hand.

"You fucked my ass, seems only fair that I fuck yours. Aren't you just a bit curious to see if it's true - the fact men can have an even more intense orgasm with a little prostate massage?" I kept my voice low, non-threatening - seductive even. I didn't wait for an answer as I slowly pushed the plastic handle in. He winced away. Whoops. My bad. Should have used a little lubrication or spit to make it easier for him. I pulled out slowly and pushed back in - a motion I kept repeating until he started to sigh. "Is that nice?" I asked.

"Yes," he sighed. His tone was weird - a cross between a man being pleasured and a man fearful for his own life. Pathetic.

"Want me to carry on?"

"Yes."

"Want me to hit that fabled g-spot?"

"Yes."

* * * * *

With the knife against Harry's throat still, I reached into the bag and pulled out a large black dildo. Not just any dildo though. This one had been modified. The end sharpened to a point. I threw the knife to the other side of the warehouse - just in case Harry suddenly found the strength to make a grab for it when I put it on the floor - and rolled Harry onto

142

his front. He screamed out in pain but I ignored him. I gobbed down onto the dildo and gave it a quick wank with my hand - to get the spit all over it, ensuring the whole tool was slippery. Perfect. Then - with no warning - I stabbed down onto Harry's rectum as hard as I could. The dildo went straight into his ass with no problems - no doubt thanks to both the lube and the fact it had been sharpened to a point. Once again - Harry screamed out. He was feeling what Tom had already experienced.

* * * * *

I pulled the handle of the knife out again and quickly span it around in my hand before thrusting back into Tom's ass with the sharp point. He screamed so loudly I thought the whole cul-de-sac was going to wake up and come investigating. Didn't stop me though as I started fucking his ass as hard and deeply as I could.

"You like that, bitch?" I screamed as my motions became more frenzied. Soon both the mattress, the sheets, Tom and I were saturated in blood. At this point, realising our time was coming to an end, I ran the second knife across his throat. A fine jet stream of blood burst from the major artery I'd successfully sliced through as he started to gargle - the sweet sounds of a dying man.

* * * * *

"Don't you dare pass out, you motherfucker!" I screamed at Harry as I continued to fuck his ass. I wasn't done with him. I had one more trick up my sleeve. One more for him to enjoy before I'd finally let him die.

I pulled the sharpened dildo out of his ass and threw it close to where the knife had landed. I knew it would have done some damage but even I was a little shocked by the amount of blood coming out. Looking at it - it wouldn't be long before he bled to death. And whilst it wouldn't be the nicest way for him to go - I had something even better up my sleeve.

"Don't you dare fucking pass out. I'm not done with you yet. Cunt! We're not done!" I climbed to my feet and hurried out to the back room once more - the final tool I'd need for the evening was in there, waiting for this moment. I couldn't help but smile when I walked into the room and saw it. Right there, on the floor, where I'd left it. I'd been waiting for this for a long time. A weird feeling rushing through me; I can't wait to get started and yet, at the same time, I want to delay it because I know - once we get going - it's over. No one survives this for more than a couple of seconds. No one.

KILLING HARRY

I looked at Tom's corpse from the foot of the bed where I was standing. The blood still dripping from my turned-on body. I was numb. It surprised me, this feeling. I thought I'd feel - I don't know - maybe a little 'good' for killing him. The pain he had put me through, the suffering I had endured...I thought I'd feel a little satisfaction for killing him. Maybe I will do when the adrenalin stops? Maybe - at that point - things will be better? I paused as I gave it a little more thought - no, I won't. I don't feel satisfaction because I know he is still out there. Harry. All the time he is out there I won't feel what I yearn to feel. It'll just consume me. I need to find him. I need to finish this.

I remembered what Tom had said about his mobile phone. Harry's number was on it. All I had to do was text him, let him know I needed to meet up...Let him know I'd...I smiled as a plan formed in my mind...I'd tell him I had seen me - the girl that got away - and that we needed to talk. That would get him out from whatever rock he was hiding under. That would do it.

I hurried from the room and down the stairs. A quick look around and I soon stumbled across Tom's mobile phone - on charge just as he'd told me it was. Another smile. I picked it up - pulling it from the charger's lead - and immediately started scanning through the mobile phone until I came across the number I was seeking. There it was. 07557980571. All I had to do was send him a text...Tell him to meet me and that's it...I could have the revenge I yearned for. I could stop him from doing this to anyone else again. I could make him feel everything I had felt on that night. Let him know what people experienced just so he could earn a little extra money.

I felt my blood start to boil as I remembered the night and thought about the experiences other girls had suffered. He needs to suffer. He needs to feel pain. He needs to feel what we had felt. And then - and only then - he needs to die.

I slid the phone into my pocket and hurried back up the stairs to fetch the knives. I grabbed them from the bed and went back down the stairs. Night would be turning to day soon and I really can't be around here for morning commuters to see leaving the property. I needed to sneak out just as I had sneaked in. In the kitchen I suddenly stopped dead; my attention caught by something sitting on the side - on the kitchen table to be more specific. Something that hadn't been there when I first had walked in. Something he must have brought home with him, when he returned from dropping the prostitute off...Something which would surely come in handy...

* * * * *

"Thank you, Tom..." I said (to myself) as I lifted the heavy chainsaw off the floor. I wasn't sure whether it was in Tom's house for a legitimate reason or whether it was part of their side-line business operations. I was hoping it was for the latter because - if that were the case - Harry was about to experience what other people had been forced to endure. Although, to be honest, it's not the end of the world if it's a virgin tool to this lifestyle. It'll still be fun. It'll still be a fitting way to end his unpleasant life.

I walked back through to the main part of the warehouse and was surprised to see that, despite his horrific injuries, he was trying his best to crawl towards the exit. A waste of energy if you ask me because - looking at him - there's no way he'd get much further than the door before passing out (again). I strolled up behind him holding the chainsaw with two hands due to the weight of it. How people can use these machines for long beats me - so damned heavy.

"Where are you going?" I asked him - a hint of delight in my tone at the fact he was clearly desperate to survive. The 'delight' coming from the fact that despite his wants - I knew he wasn't going to survive. I knew that, within the next five minutes, he'd be dead. He didn't answer me. Too busy concentrating on fighting through the unbearable pain to answer me. Too busy trying to crawl his way, dragging his dead legs, towards his supposed freedom. Deluded man. There is no freedom. "Recognise this?" I asked him. I lifted the chainsaw up. He didn't turn around to see what I was referring to. He just kept going - making slow progress yet still trying. "I took it from Tom's house. I was hoping you could tell me whether he was going to use it for, I don't know, some pruning perhaps or whether it was part of your business. A tool you guys used. In fact, if you could have a look at everything I brought with me tonight - even the bag, I'd be grateful if you could say whether you've seen it before. Whether you've used it on other women before. You see, I took it all from Tom's house..."

Under the table, where I'd found the chainsaw, I'd seen the bag. Curiosity had got the better of me and I had had to take a look; had to see if there was anything else that would be as useful as the chainsaw. Imagine my delight when I had found the hammer and the chains. It was then I had formulated the plan. I would text Harry - pretending to be Tom - and warn him I'd seen me. I wasn't dead. I was still out there and that could only spell trouble for the pair of them. I sent him a text saying that we needed to meet up to discuss it as - details - it couldn't be talked about on the phone. I left it at that. Too many details, I thought, and he'd get suspicious. I pressed 'send' and within a couple of minutes, despite the time, I received a reply. Harry. It simply asked where and when Tom wanted to meet.

And that's how we ended up back here - the same warehouse where they had based my attack. It made sense. I suggested – by text - to Harry that we needed to meet the following evening and gave him a time. Clearly it was safe to carry out the meeting here. Had it not been safe, they'd never have brought me here on that night. For all I know - one of them actually owned the warehouse and this was the only purpose it served; four walls to hide the torturous events which unfolded under the roof. That was - of course - best case scenario but even if they didn't own it and someone did swing by to see what I had done (or was doing) - who cares? So I'd go to prison. Locked up for seeking the justice I believed these fucks deserved. My life is over anyway. It was the moment they first touched me. I was fine with going to prison. I really was. It wasn't as though I was trying to hide the crimes I was committing. I didn't care if they were discovered. Hell, I wanted them to be found. I wanted them to serve as a warning to the fucks out there, like Tom and Harry, who believe they have the right to carry out such atrocities the way they did with me. I want them to know that people aren't afraid to stand up to them and that - if they're not careful - they'll end up as the bodies I left behind.

Thinking back to Tom's house - as I continued to laugh at Harry struggling to make any progress on the floor - the chainsaw, hammer and chains weren't the only things I had taken from the seemingly nice family home. Knowing the pain I wanted to inflict, I had gone back up to where his corpse was slowly rotting and grabbed the knives I'd used to kill him. A quick look around, in the drawers, to see if there was anything else of use and I found the sex toys. More than I needed - dildos of various shapes and sizes, butt-plugs, penis enlarger; he had the whole collection. I took the biggest of dildos and the butt-plug and that was it. Without tidying up behind me I ran from his house whilst still in the witching hour. Sticking close to the walls I hurried back to my car in the next cul-de-sac as quickly as I could, considering the excess weight of the bag over my shoulder and the chainsaw in my hands. I threw the stuff in the boot and high-tailed it out of there; back to my own apartment for the last time.

"It had been the first time I'd gone back to my apartment since that night," I told Harry for no other reason than completion of the story. The last piece of the picture I felt he deserved to see. "The latex cat-suit, this one, the one you made me wear that night - it was on the floor where I'd dropped it when getting changed whilst the good samaritan was waiting for me. Seemed fitting to wear it for the meeting, don't you think?"

Harry still didn't answer me - still too busy trying to make his feeble escape. Considering how far he'd managed to drag himself I couldn't help but wonder whether he knew it was pointless. Did he really believe he was getting anywhere?

"I'm looking forward to this," I told him, "to killing you. The only thing that bothers me is the fact I know you're not the only ones who deserve to die. The other men - the voyeurs on the set - they deserve to die as well. If they're happy to pay to watch someone get tortured and killed then they deserve everything they have coming their way. The same as you and Tom. I hate the thought of them thinking they've gotten away with it. Not sure if Tom was telling the truth when he told me you don't keep their details but - just so you know - when you're dead I'm going to take that driving licence in your wallet, the one I found when I stripped you - and I'm going to search your house from top to bottom. Any

PORN

signs of these fucks, or any of the people who like to log onto your website...I'll go after them. I'll do everything I can to find them and hurt them. If Tom was telling the truth and you do not have the details anywhere, or I can't find them - well I guess that's the end of the road. They get away with it. At least I can go to my grave knowing you didn't though. I can die knowing you're rotting in a special place in Hell. Just as you deserve."

Harry screamed out. Nothing in particular. No apology. No insult. Just a scream.

Those last few hours - in the apartment - before heading out here to prepare the warehouse for Harry's arrival...They were spent thinking about all the things I wanted to do to him. The chainsaw being the grand finale. Ideas about fucking his ass with a dildo - sharpened to a point whilst counting down the hours, the hammer to beat his body to a broken mess, the tying him to the pillar - everything was considered and planned. I even got the padlocks from my suitcases to ensure he couldn't break free from the chains.

* * * * *

I parked my car around the corner from the warehouse. I didn't want Harry showing up only to get spooked by a strange car parked out front. It was two hours prior to our meeting. Again, if Harry showed up early - it wouldn't have mattered. I'd already be there, waiting. I couldn't see him showing up as early as this. Maybe thirty minutes or so before the scheduled meeting but not two hours.

I had carried the stuff through to the warehouse - climbing in via a broken window at the back of the property - and dumped it all in the room out back. The main floor of the warehouse was empty other than a little litter in the corner. The bed, which was used during our time together was missing, and obviously there were no signs of the cameras. Of course not - they wouldn't leave either behind. Luckily I had brought my own camera along. Sure it wasn't as fancy as the ones they had used but - even so - it was better than nothing. Something, at least, to capture our moment together. Something, at least, to permit me the opportunity to upload to their sordid website at a later date (if I could figure it out or find his computer).

The plan was relatively straight forward. With my possessions stashed, I was going to lie in wait, just to the side of the warehouse door. There was only one 'normal' way in and one shutter entrance so it wouldn't have been hard to hear which entrance he was going to use. I'd wait for him to step into the building and I'd wait for the door to shut. Then - and only then - I'd rush him and hit him with the hammer. Hopefully one blow would be enough to knock him out but worst case it would be enough to stun him - and a second blow, maybe third, would get him unconscious. Actually, the worst case was the one hit could kill him outright but I didn't have any choice but to try. After all - there was no other way I'd be able to subdue him.

God I hope it doesn't kill him.

Only now I was in position, patiently waiting, did I start to panic about my plan. My brain playing the game of 'what if'. What if he sees me before I have a chance to hit him? Considering I am only pressed up flat against the wall beside the door he'll be using - it's possible he will see me. What if he manages to wrestle the hammer from me? What if he doesn't come alone? What if there are more people with him? I won't be able to fight them all off. My heart was beating hard and fast when the door handle finally turned.

This is it.

The moment I've been waiting for.

I gripped the hammer tightly and prepared myself.

* * * *

"You know the rest," I told Harry. "You went down like a sack of shit. I thought I had killed you. I only realised I hadn't when I felt your pulse. Out for the count as planned. Long enough for me to chain you to the pillar - no easy feat I can tell you. Long enough to change into the latex cat-suit. Long enough to carry on dreaming about what I was going to do to you. Long enough to think of this moment." I smiled. We were here. The moment I'd been waiting for.

I powered up the chainsaw. The loud roar of the motor as the saw span around in a blur. I started to laugh as I inched it closer and closer to his rectum. He started screaming before it even touched his skin. Music to my ears that - despite the roar of the chainsaw's blade - I could still hear the screams perfectly.

"Fuck you!" I shouted as I pressed the saw into his flesh. His scream changed pitch entirely - a pitch I'd never heard before as the skin tore from his body in splatterings upon splatterings of blood. I screamed again, "FUCK YOU!" I pushed down with the chainsaw; no resistance from his skin as it sliced through him as though his body were nothing. Skin turned to muscle which turned to bone. I pulled out slightly before pushing back in and pulling out again; fucking his ass with the heavy-duty tip of the saw. I could have gone all the way through his body had I chosen to do so but - no - that was too easy. I pulled the chainsaw out and kicked his body over so he was on his back; cock-side up. His body was convulsing as blood poured from behind him onto the floor. He's practically dead so I can but only hope he still feels this. I pressed the chainsaw down onto his genitals and let the motor do its work. By the time I lifted the saw back up again his penis was nothing but shredded skin. No scream from him though. I looked at his face, his body still violently shaking, and his eyes had rolled to the back of his head. Blood and drool spilling from his mouth. That fucking face. I could still picture the look on his face when he was unchaining me from the bed, the smug fucking grin as he whispered that I had my freedom now...With no hesitation I took the chainsaw to his face and slice in an upward motion - careful not to go too deep. I didn't want to take his head off. Just his face. It came off in one satisfying chunk and left nothing behind but a perfect cross-section of the inside of his head...His mouth (now silent), his tongue hanging there, his eye-sockets with sliced eyeballs still sitting inside and his brain - the front section sliced off along with his facial features. I killed the power of the chainsaw in time to hear his final gargled breath. Pretty sure that he was already dead. Pretty sure. The breath, no doubt, a final escape of air previously sucked in. Nothing more and nothing less. A shame though for I'd have loved for him to feel all of that. He deserved to.

I dropped the bloodied chainsaw at my feet and just stood there a moment. I wiped my face with the back of my hand. I must have looked a state, the blood splashed everywhere with each slice and dice. I could feel it in my hair, matting it up. I could feel it running down my bosom, cheeks...I looked around the room and couldn't quite believe the distance the spray had travelled.

With no warning I screamed out loud - as loud as I could - and dropped to my knees and burst into tears. I allowed myself the luxury of tears for a minute or two before I slapped myself in the face, "Stop it!" Still crying. I slapped myself harder, "Stop it! Pull yourself together! Stop it!" I covered my hands with my eyes. A little bit of darkness, a little bit of blocking out the reality of where I am. A little time to gather my senses and calm down.

"You're pathetic!"

A voice. I jumped at the sound of it. I recognised who it was but I couldn't bring myself to look. It couldn't be real. Must be in my head. Must be. There's no other possible solution.

"Open your eyes, cunt!"

It was Harry. His tone was filled with venom. But it can't be. It can't be him. I slowly peeled my hands away from my eyes and turned to look at him. He was there - staring at me from the floor where I'd left him. Not a drop of blood on him. In fact, he looked perfect. Not a hair out of place.

"What the fuck is this? You're trying to fucking kill me? What? You a fucking vigilante now?"

"You aren't real. You're dead. I killed you..."

"I said - open your eyes, you fucking cunt! OPEN THEM!"

My vision faded to black. I blinked repeatedly until I could get it back. A struggle. I tried to rub my eyes - to try and help the process - but couldn't. I couldn't move.

"I can't move," I cried. Panic was starting to set in. And my head...My head...Such a headache.

"Of course you can't. Open your fucking eyes..."

Slowly my vision focused. I realised I was standing up. More so - I was looking at the floor. I tried to move again. I couldn't. My hands...My feet...Chained. What the hell is going on?

"What's happening?" I stuttered.

A hand went around my throat and startled to throttle me. I looked up. Harry was standing in front of me. Fully dressed. Unharmed. How is this possible? As vision started to fade again, I noticed the hammer - my hammer - in Harry's other hand. He relaxed his grip on my neck and started to laugh.

"What? Did you think you were going to hit me with this? Was that your plan? Hit me with the hammer and - I'm guessing - chain me to the pillar like this? Is that how it was going to be?" Harry started to laugh at me. "How'd that work out for you? Jesus - you got away from us, you were safe. We thought you were dead and yet - here you are. You could have got away with it. You could have just got on with your life and put the past in the past. But you didn't...And now you're here." He paused as he looked me up and down, "I hope you don't mind - whilst you were out cold...I put you in the outfit. Found it out back with a whole load of goodies...What? Those meant for me?" He glanced to the side. I followed his gaze and noticed the chainsaw on the floor, next to the bag of toys. "Oh - and I found that too...Thought I'd set it up for you," he nodded to the other side of me. I turned. My camcorder was set-up recording.

My brain ached as though it was on the verge of breaking; straining, trying to remember what had happened.

* * * * *

I was in position, patiently waiting, and starting to panic about my plan. My brain playing the game of 'what if'. What if he sees me before I have a chance to hit him? Considering I am only pressed up flat against the wall by the door he'll be using - it's possible he will see me. What if he manages to wrestle the hammer from me? What if he hasn't come alone? What if there are more people with him? I won't be able to fight them all off. My heart was beating hard and fast when the door handle finally turned.

This is it.

The moment I've been waiting for.

I gripped the hammer tightly and prepared myself.

Harry stepped into the warehouse. Immediately I screamed and dashed towards him, the hammer raised high in the air. He span, on the spot, and jumped when he saw me. I swung the hammer downward towards his skull and screamed again when he caught a hold of my wrist; the hammer inches from the side of his temple.

"Get the fuck off me!" I screamed.

I saw in his face that he recognised me, as I struggled to break free from his grip. With little effort he snatched the hammer from me and swung it towards my head. I tried to get away but tripped over my own feet. I landed on my ass as the hammer smashed past my head, mere inches away. Harry wasted no time, he stepped towards me with the hammer raised high in the air again; ready for another blow…I braced myself.

OUR LAST SHOOT (PART 2)

I started to cry as I continued to struggle against the restraints. Harry was still laughing at me. He composed himself long enough to address me once more.

"How did you get his phone?"

I didn't answer him.

"I'll ask you again - how did you get my friend's phone? I mean - I'm guessing you sent me that text message…What with you standing here and him being nowhere around? And - whilst you're explaining that…" He looked across to the chainsaw, "Pretty sure I recognise that too."

"Fuck you."

Harry didn't say anything. You could see he was putting things together in his own mind; working out what had happened. He knew I had sent the text, he knew I had the chainsaw - probably even recognised the bag I had with me. After what seemed an age, he looked me directly in the eye and asked, "Is my friend alive?"

"No more than my friend."

He nodded. He understood. It didn't need to be spelt out.

"How'd you find where he was?" he asked. His tone was low. Almost as though he was upset by his friend's death. People like him feel upset?

"Fluke."

"How so?"

"Came here and just happened to bump into him. He picked a woman up...Took her to his place. I just followed."

Harry smiled, "Ah. Yes. He could never say no to the ladies. That certainly is a fluke sighting." He paused. "How'd he die?"

"Let me out of here," I said, "and I'll show you."

Harry smiled again - amused by my attempt to gain freedom.

"We won't be undoing those chains again," he said. The smile faded from his face. "Your agent - Frank - he didn't point you towards us then?"

"What?"

"First time we had used him. Would hate to think he sold us out after taking that money..."

My brain ached when I realised everything I thought I knew from earlier conversations with Harry was nothing but my imagination playing tricks on me whilst I laid unconscious on the floor. My brain told me Frank was innocent and that what I did to him in his apartment was a mistake? Weird - I was unconscious and yet I felt nothing but guilt when I realised I'd potentially infected him for nothing. Ruined the life of an innocent man.

"I knew he couldn't be fucking trusted," Harry sighed. "Okay. Well. Fine. We can deal with him later. Won't be the first time we've had to set people straight." Harry started to laugh, "You tried to protect him by lying about how you found Tom?" He shook his head, "He set you up for this. He put you in our path. Easily bought. Greedy man. Yet, just because he told you where to find Tom, you try and protect him?" He shrugged, "Well I don't get it but each to their own."

I realised Harry hadn't believed my story about how I had stumbled across Tom. He thought my agent had sold them out. I won't correct him. When he is finished with me - he'll go after Frank. He'll give him what he deserved.

"Anyway - not important - we'll deal with him later. Now…We have a little problem with what we're going to do with you…"

I struggled against the restraints again. It was obvious I wasn't getting out of them. Harry took a step back and watched. A smile on his face. Satisfaction in knowing I wasn't going anywhere.

"Well…" he looked over to the chainsaw, "…seems a shame to waste that. I mean, you went to the trouble of bringing it to the party. May as well have a play, hey? And - I'll be honest - it looks great on camera." He nodded towards the camera again.

"Fuck you."

He walked over to the chainsaw and picked it up. He returned to me with a sadistic grin on his face. "I'm surprised you could even carry this. It's pretty heavy." He held the tip of it up to my neck, "I don't suppose you know how to turn it on do you?" he started to play with the various controls on the chainsaw. I closed my eyes, waiting for the saw to start spinning...to start cutting through me. My heart was racing. He laughed. "Come on," he lowered the chainsaw to the floor, "I'm just fucking about. I can't kill you. Not yet at least. You see - I've made a few phone calls and there are quite a few people who want to watch your final moments." He smiled, "Full circle. Back to where our relationship first begun."

I started to cry.

"Don't waste those precious tears," he said, wiping them carefully from my cheek. "A few people are paying good money to see those...Here...Maybe I can make things better for you...Maybe I can help you calm down..." He ran his fingers down my cheek and gave me a wink. His eyes distracted by the shiny material of the latex cat-suit, "You have no idea how happy I am you brought this with you...The way it hugs your figure, sticks to your skin...So fucking hot." His fingers ran from my cheek down my neck and onto the rubber material of the suit.

"Don't fucking touch me," I hissed. I fought the tears back. For a minute, just a second, I thought I had failed. I thought Harry had won. He was getting what he originally wanted from me. My death and a lot of money. At least - that's what I thought for a split second. But he hasn't won. I still have a chance of winning this. I still have a chance of ruining him. All I need to do is to put on a poor show for the camera and his cronies. Make sure they're dissatisfied. An unhappy customer is not a repeat customer.

"Look at you - all brave and shit...We're going to have fun with you...Oh, and on that note, thank you so much for getting me to meet you so early. If we're careful, if we take things slowly, then we have the whole night."

Without thinking twice I spat directly in his face. I started to laugh as my dribble snaked its way down his face until he used the back of his hand to wipe it away.

"For your information...Just because we're going to use the whole night up to have our fun with you...Don't be fooled into thinking any of it will be pleasant. You are going to hurt for every single second. You understand me?"

Before I had the chance to answer he fired the chainsaw up. The sudden roar of the teeth all spinning around the axle made me jump. He raised the chainsaw up close to my face. I closed my eyes as the chainsaw inched ever closer to my face. I didn't scream though. Not once. Not even close.

Epilogue

THE DAY I DIED

Harry had put the chainsaw down and was going through the bag I'd packed. He wasn't saying anything - just actually making a strange 'grunt' noise from his throat. I had stopped trying to escape from my restraints. It was clear they weren't going anywhere - just as it was clear they hadn't been going anywhere in my unconscious dreams where I got to watch Harry struggle beneath them. Harry. It should be him in my place. It shouldn't be me. It's not fair that I'm here. I don't deserve it. He does.

The door opened and my heart skipped a beat as a group of men came in. None of them were saying anything. None of them greeted Harry. They all just walked in - in silence - with their eyes fixed upon me in a way which turned my skin cold.

Harry stood up, "Gentlemen. I was beginning to think you weren't coming." He turned around and pointed to the chainsaw. "Look at what she brought to the party."

"Nice."

"...And not just that. She brought a bag with her. Look."
Harry grabbed the bag, from the side, and emptied it over
the floor. The sharpened dildo, the hammer, the small butt-
plug - everything I had planned to use on Harry - fell onto the
hard floor. He kicked the small butt-plug across the room - as
though disgusted by the sight of it, "Don't think we'll be
using that pathetic excuse for an anal toy." He looked at the
men's faces. They were suitably impressed. "So here's what
I'm thinking," he said, "you each don a mask, you each fuck
her any way, whichever way you want...Cover her in cum...I
mean literally drench the cunt and then...When we're
done...We torture her until you want some more.
Gentleman, we have the whole night and we're going to
make it count."

"Can't very well fuck her in the chains," one of the men
pointed out.

"You remember what happened the last time," Harry gave
the man a wink. "I thought it best we stop a repeat
performance of the last time..." He pointed towards the
hammer. "Who wants the honours?"

A large burly man stepped forward from the rest of the
group. His eyes were fixed directly on me as he said, "I'll do
it."

"Be my guest - consider it a bonus after the troubles we had
with the flighty cunt the last time," Harry sneered. He turned
to me and whispered, "You might want to brace yourself -
this is going to hurt."

The stranger picked the hammer up and stormed towards me; a look of both hatred and anticipation on his face. I wanted to ask what I had done to him, what women in general had done, to warrant such a look but I knew he wouldn't answer. He (they) didn't want to hear my questions or even communicate with me. They just wanted me to scream before I died.

Harry stopped him, "If I were you I wouldn't walk any further...Don't want to appear on camera without your masks do you? Remember, I don't edit before I upload. I want the viewers to experience exactly what you experienced. No special effects, no cutting away..."

The large man turned to one of the smaller in the group, "Where are the masks?"

The small man held up a rucksack. "I have them." He opened the bag and distributed white masks around the room. By the time they had all put them on, Harry included, they looked like Michael Myers from Halloween. Blank, expressionless faces, black eyes. I didn't need to see their faces to know they were smiling though. I could tell.

"Okay?" the large man looked to Harry for his approval.

Harry slowly nodded. He gestured, with his hand, for the man to do what needed to be done. The man needed no further invitation.

He stormed towards me and swung the hammer directly into the side of my leg. I tried not to scream. I tried not to give them the satisfaction. Not quite silent. Something came from my mouth. Some kind of noise. Not a scream though. The man turned to Harry, as though confused by the lack of reaction. Harry shrugged and gestured towards my other leg. The man nodded and swung the hammer around to my other leg - another noise from my mouth but still not a scream. The pain was intense and - had it not been for the chains holding me in place - I would have dropped to the floor.

Harry handed the padlock key to one of the other men.

I heard him whisper, "She probably won't be running anywhere now."

The second man hurried forward and went to work on the keys whilst the large man with the hammer just stayed standing in front of me - ready to stop me if I dared run (or try and run).

"Lock the door," Harry instructed a third man. The third man did as he was told.

The chains dropped to the floor, as did I. I landed heavily on my knees and yelped out in pain. Still not a scream. I won't give it to them. I won't give them the scream they so desperately yearn for. I looked up to the large man. The hammer was still in his hand but now - so was his penis, in his other hand. He was stroking it hard. I could hear his breathing from behind the mask, getting heavier as he became more turned on. I won't beg him to leave me alone. I won't beg him to hit me with the hammer and just end my life. I won't. I won't give them the satisfaction. They want some fight but they won't get it from me. Won't even spit at him despite a strong urge.

The second man appeared from behind the pillar. He dropped the padlocks to the floor and started to undo his trousers. A quick look to the other men and they were doing the same; all fumbling at their belts. Even Harry was gearing up to join in.

A sudden thought crossed my mind, a fleeting thought which brought a smile to my face. Even when the large man pushed me onto my back and forcefully parted my legs before fumbling at the zipper on the cat-suit - giving him access to my dry pussy - I couldn't help but smile. Here they all were - getting ready to fuck me - all of them closing in on me...None of them were reaching for condoms.

* * * * *

I was sitting in the doctor's office. He was talking but I wasn't hearing anything that he said. My eyes fixed on the wall. The wall. Various posters on varied subjects - most dealing with health issues such as diabetes and how to keep a healthy heart...One, on the bottom left of the group...One mentioned sexually transmitted diseases.

"Did you hear me?" the doctor asked. I didn't answer him. "Miss Sheldon?" his voice was a little louder this time.

"I'm sorry - what?" I suddenly came 'to'. I looked at him. He looked concerned. God only knows how I looked to him.

"Did you hear what I've been telling you?"

I nodded. I heard. HIV. My life was over. Even if the medication helped to keep it at bay, even if they worked wonders at extending your life expectancy - the stigma attached to the illness...Friends and family wouldn't understand. The true friends - and my family - they'd pretend to understand. They'd pretend to be okay with it and pretend to be supportive but I know, deep down, they wouldn't be. My life - as I knew it - was over.

* * * * *

The first man screamed out with pleasure as he ejaculated deep inside of me. I was staring at the blank expression on the white mask - wondering what his face was doing underneath, wondering whether my poisoned cunt had made him happy, wondering how he'd feel when the disease takes a hold of his body...Wondering what his family and friends would think? He moved off from me and the next man climbed on top. Another white mask. Another blank expression. Another erect penis. Another life about to change forever. They took it in turn to each ejaculate inside of me - one after the other.

I didn't scream.

I smiled.

THE END

MATT SHAW

www.facebook.com/mattshawpublications

www.mattshawpublications.co.uk

Printed in Great Britain
by Amazon

80934302R00098